DARK FUGITIVE

Just before Christmas, Laura sets out for her cottage in the Pennine fells. *En route,* through worsening weather, she catches a news bulletin about a brutal killing and this increases her determination to seek refuge in her remote, childhood home. However, Laura finds her cottage occupied by a man who claims to be a stranded walker. When she finds herself snowed in with Julian North, a man she believes could be the suspected wife-killer, she soon begins to doubt her own integrity – can you fall in love with a murderer?

DARK FUGITIVE

Dark Fugitive

by

Clare Benedict

Dales Large Print Books
Long Preston, North Yorkshire,
BD23 4ND, England.

British Library Cataloguing in Publication Data.

Benedict, Clare
    Dark fugitive.

    A catalogue record of this book is
    available from the British Library

    ISBN   1-84262-258-7 pbk

First published in Great Britain in 1992 by Robert Hale Limited

Published in Large Print 2003 by arrangement with
Robert Hale Ltd.

Dales Large Print is an imprint of Library Magna Books Ltd.

Printed and bound in Great Britain by
T.J. (International) Ltd., Cornwall, PL28 8RW

ONE

'Don't look so surprised, Steve, you know that I always find you out sooner or later.'

The expensively dressed woman pushed past him into the living-room and then stopped and looked at Laura with an expression of contempt.

'My God, you usually have better taste – this one's completely raw and unsophisticated!'

Steve remained by the door which he had just opened; he was aghast and embarrassed. Laura watched his reaction with growing unease.

'Well, aren't you going to tell the poor girl who I am? No, I can see that it's up to me, as usual.'

She had been glancing coldly at him as she said this but now she turned her attention back to Laura. 'Just in case you haven't already guessed, let me introduce myself, I'm Maxine Fraser – Steve's wife.'

After they had gone Laura had relived the

scene over and over in her mind. She gripped the arms of the chair as she remembered the woman's face twisted with rage and spite, but she still found it difficult to believe what had followed.

Steve, who should have defended her, had said nothing. He had snatched up his coat and gone scurrying after his wife, leaving Laura without a backward glance and slamming the door behind him.

At first she had thought that he would come back as soon as he could and explain everything. But she had waited in vain – he had not returned. Laura realized, now, that he never would.

Now, hours later, the wind spattered rain against the windows of her top floor, riverside flat and she could hear the insistent beat of disco music from the nightclub below. The quayside was a changed world after dark and now, in mid-December, the restaurants and winebars were already festooned with Christmas decorations.

Laura went to the window and looked down. The reflections of the coloured fairy-lights strung around the windows shone like jewels on the wet cobblestones and spilled over on to the dark waters of the river.

She loved living here by the river. This had been Laura's home since her parents had died. She had found it herself and spent weeks decorating and furnishing it until it was just right. She had thought of it as her special haven. Now it was spoilt. Maxine had seen to that.

It was long past midnight when she packed her belongings into her small car. The eating-places had closed but the nightclubs were still open and music and laughter drifted across the cold waters of the river from 'The Princess', the converted North Sea ferry, moored under the Tyne Bridge.

Laura's car was parked in a small courtyard reserved for residents of the flats. She eased it gently forward through the old archway and out on to the road, avoiding a couple of merrymakers who burst out of a doorway singing carols. They were draped in tinsel streamers. There were two weeks to go but, for them, it seemed that the Christmas celebrations had already started.

Once away from the riverside, the graceful streets were hushed and dark. As Laura began to leave Newcastle by the West Road there was no glimmer of light in the eastern skies behind her. She wondered, fancifully, how fast she would have to drive to escape the new day completely and keep the night wrapped around her like a cloak.

She had packed her clothes swiftly and emptied the contents of the kitchen cupboards and the fridge into cardboard boxes. A few trips down in the lift to the back door which opened into the courtyard and then a final, hasty glance around her flat and she was away.

The delicate pattern of raindrops on the windscreen was blurring and turning into rivulets as the rain became heavier. Laura turned on the windscreen wipers. Their regular swishing was the only noise in the warm darkness of the car and, gradually, her nerves eased enough to allow her to concentrate on her driving.

She felt safe, enclosed. Her car was a time-capsule transporting her to a place and time where nobody would find her and nobody could hurt her.

Strangely, she didn't feel tired. She was a good driver and she reacted automatically to the gradually worsening conditions. Soon she found the sheer effort needed to keep going pushed the recent drama to the back of her mind.

But, then, in an unguarded moment,

everything came flooding back. Maxine's face sprang out before her eyes as if from a three-dimensional screen.

'Don't think I'll forget this. For a start I'll see you never work again. If your boss, Chris Martin, wants to keep my father's contract, he'd better not submit your designs – and that goes for any other firm that would be foolish enough to employ you!'

Laura blinked and the image was gone. She gripped the wheel and concentrated on the road but she could still hear Maxine's strident tones ringing round the car.

She reached forward and switched on the radio, finding the soothing sounds of an all-night music programme.

Then she noticed that the rain was beginning to turn into snow. The snowflakes appeared magically from the darkened sky and hurled themselves against the car. The windscreen wipers had to work harder than ever, bending and complaining as they pushed the soft white substance from one side to the other until it melted.

When daybreak finally caught up with her it revealed a bleak, windswept landscape divided by ancient stone boundary walls.

The café at the service station shone out

like a beacon to welcome weary travellers. Laura's head was aching violently and her eyes were heavy with lack of sleep. She realized she would have to stop and refresh herself.

She parked the car and paused to stare out over the fields. The ploughed furrows, edged with snow, rose towards the horizon where black elms raised bare branches towards a grey sky streaked with crimson.

She caught her breath. Even in her state of misery and exhaustion she could appreciate the cruel beauty of the winter landscape.

Just before she turned off the car radio she caught an early morning news bulletin.

'–the latest development in the so-called "Belgravia murder". A police spokesman says they still have not been able to make contact with the victim's husband, Julian North, who is understood to have returned to England on the night of the killing.

'Mr North is well known for his prize-winning television news coverage and, if anyone knows his whereabouts, they should inform the police immediately.'

Laura switched off the radio and got out of the car. She was sickened by this glimpse of a world of hate and violence and she became more determined than ever to seek refuge in the cottage.

For, although this journey had not been planned, Laura knew exactly where she was going – to the cottage where she had spent the happiest times of her life.

Her parents had bought it when she was a child so that they would have a base in England in between her father's tours of duty abroad.

Her father had had money independent of his army pay so, although she was orphaned, Laura had no financial worries. But most of all she had the cottage, full of secure, loving memories, and that was where she needed to be now.

The café was clean and warm and the tea freshly made. The hot, sweet liquid revived her and Laura surprised herself by managing to eat a couple of rounds of toast and honey.

The only other customers were two lorry drivers, obviously regulars, who sat at the next table devouring large platesful of bacon, sausage and eggs. They kept up a flow of jokey chatter with the young waitress.

The latter was probably about the same age as Laura and, although she was yawning sleepily, she gave an impression of wholesome cleanliness in her blue-checked overall.

Laura glanced at her own reflection in the window next to her. The image that stared back looked crumpled and tired. After she had paid for her meal she went into the powder room to freshen up.

She examined herself more closely in the mirror on the tiled wall above the sink. There were shadows under her green eyes and her perfect, oval face looked drawn and weary. Normally her skin glowed soft and creamy, with a faint dusting of freckles across her fine, straight nose but now her complexion was dull and uniformly grey.

She washed her face and patted it dry with paper towels. She rubbed some cream into her skin and then she set about brushing her thick, copper-coloured hair. Once it was tamed, she tucked it up into her green angora hat.

She looked at herself critically. She saw a face that was young and vulnerable; she could see how someone as glamorous as Maxine would think her raw and unsophisticated, but she was content with her own image and, feeling more presentable, she stepped back into the café.

The chat and the laughter had stopped.

The two customers and the waitress were staring at the television set mounted above the counter. The chef had come out of the kitchen to join them.

One of the breakfast-time television programmes had started and the screen showed an elegant London square totally disrupted by the assembled media.

A woman reporter, dressed in a sheepskin coat to guard against the chill morning air, faced the camera and talked with barely concealed excitement.

'–and in the last few minutes we have learned that there is evidence to suggest that the victim's husband, well-known television reporter Julian North, has definitely been in the house since he returned from South East Asia but, soon after that, he disappeared and, at this moment no one knows his exact whereabouts.

'All the police will tell me is that they do not think he can have left the country because they have effectively closed off all ports and airports.

'They have not ruled out the possibility that someone may be giving him refuge.'

Briefly, Laura thought about the desperate man and she wondered if he had, indeed, found a safe refuge as everyone imagined.

She almost had a fellow feeling for someone on the run, someone as unhappy as she was. Then she dismissed the thoughts angrily. Their situations were not at all similar. Julian North had probably killed his wife. He did not deserve sympathy.

Still intent on the unfolding drama on the screen, no one noticed Laura as she slipped out into the softly falling snow.

She got into her car and set out once more for her cottage in the high fells of the North Pennines.

Not much later the red Astra was climbing up the little-used road into the valley. The weak winter sun bathed the scene in an unearthly, silvery light and as Laura passed a ruined, long-deserted farmhouse she thought for the first time of the dangers of coming here alone during bad weather.

She had not expected it to be like this. The long-range weather forecast had not pre-dicted the sudden cold snap and the snow.

But even if I do get snowed in, it won't matter, Laura thought.

She had brought enough provisions to last a week or more and the coal-house behind the cottage should be full of logs for the fire. She chose not to dwell on the fact that there was no telephone.

Laura could see the cottage now, nestling against the fellside. For a moment the sunlight glinted on the windows set in the slate-grey stone and then the sun vanished behind a cloud.

By the time she drove into the old barn that was used as a garage, the sky was grey and heavy with the threat of further snow.

As soon as she opened the door of the cottage she knew something was wrong. The air inside was not as cold as it should have been and the quality of the sound was not right – not for an empty building.

She peered ahead into the shadowy interior. As her eyes grew accustomed to the dimness the usual contours of the living-room fell into place. Everything looked as it should.

Opposite she could see the door that led into the small kitchen. It was closed as she had left it last time she was here. Was there someone at the other side of that door listening intently, just as she was?

I'm imagining things because I'm tired, she thought. She stepped inside.

Immediately the door slammed shut and she was grabbed from behind. He had been waiting behind the front door. Vainly, she tried to twist around to see her attacker but the grip tightened, one strong arm slipping up towards her throat.

Laura was sure that the man intended to throttle her. Desperately she bent her head forward and sank her teeth into his wrist.

With an oath, her captor released her, at the same time hurling her forwards so that she fell on to the stone-flagged floor.

Laura was shaking but she forced herself to look up at the figure towering over her. He was standing with his back to the window so that all she could see was a powerful silhouette.

The man was tall with broad shoulders. He bent his head to examine his wrist in the weak light and then he turned to stare down at her.

She gasped in fright as she saw his eyes glinting in the dark face. His eyes were the only clue to his emotions for the rest of his facial expressions were obscured by an abundant, black beard.

With the light behind him he had the advantage and he saw a slim girl with green eyes and rich copper-coloured hair escaping from her woollen hat and falling about her face. She crouched as if she were ready to spring and, although he could see fear in her eyes, there was something else

18

there, too – anger.

He spoke first, 'I'm sorry, I didn't mean to harm you. I thought you were someone else.'

He offered her a hand to help her up but she stared at it with cold distaste and scrambled to her feet in one lithe movement. She didn't speak.

Whatever he had thought while he had watched the car coming up the valley towards the cottage, he was puzzled now. 'Who are you and what are you doing here?'

Laura was furious but she remained as composed as possible. 'I'm Laura Stewart, this is my cottage and I have every right to be here. Now who are you?'

He was taken aback. 'The Stewart girl? But I thought you were just a child!'

That was the last thing she had expected him to say. She stared at him blankly. Did she know him? No, she didn't think so – and yet, in spite of the beard which obscured his features, there was something vaguely familiar about him. Was he someone from long ago – someone who had known her parents? One of her father's army colleagues perhaps?

Laura faltered. 'Do – do you know me – or did you know my parents?'

'No, to both questions but I've walked these fells since I was a boy. I know the whereabouts of all the farms and cottages and I know who owns them. I heard your parents had been killed abroad and I thought you were still at boarding-school – or living with relatives.'

His voice was deep and reassuring and, as Laura listened, she thought it was familiar – and yet he claimed they had never met.

She realized he was staring at her expectantly. He must have asked her a question and she had missed it.

'I'm sorry, what did you say?'

'I said I didn't think anyone would mind if I took shelter here during the snowstorm. You don't, do you? Mind, I mean?'

'N-no, I suppose not...'

She studied her unexpected guest. He was wearing a grey, Shetland sweater over a green and black checked shirt, black cords and good quality walking shoes.

For the first time she noticed the rucksack behind him and to one side of the door. She saw the metal initials J.N punched into the canvas flap which buckled over the top. The man saw the direction of her glance.

'My name's Norton, by the way, John Norton. Sorry not to have introduced myself properly before. Now you're not going to turn me out in the cold, are you?'

Laura looked out of the window. It would be inhuman to send him out in this. He looked like a genuine fell walker and, even if he was unknown to her, personally, he seemed to know who she was and something about her background. 'All right, you can stay until the snow stops.'

'Good, now let's get this place warmed up.'

Laura wondered, wryly, what would have happened if she had refused him permission to stay. She doubted very much if she could have forced a man of his size to go against his will.

And there was something else niggling away in her mind – something to do with... No, she was too tired. She would have to puzzle it out later...

She allowed him to help her off with her outdoor things and lead her over towards the fireplace. Lack of sleep was catching up with her and she sat and watched, willingly, as he made the fire, using logs from the basket next to the hearth.

He was an expert. In no time at all the logs began to crackle and wisps of smoke drifted up amongst the first pale flames.

Then he stood up, suddenly, and knocked over the old, two-bar electric fire which had been standing to one side of the fireplace. Surely last time she had been here she had put that away in the cupboard under the stairs?

She bent forward to pick it up and move it out of his way and she realized it was warm. She looked up to find him watching her intently.

'I put the electric fire on before. The cottage was very cold when I arrived.'

'How – how long have you been here?'

'Oh, not much longer than you.'

'But–'

'No "buts"! You need a hot drink and so do I. I've got some emergency rations – let's go into the kitchen and get a meal started. After we've eaten we'll talk all you like. Good idea?'

She started to follow him to the kitchen and then she remembered her boxes of food and her belongings were still in the car. She went over to the front door and was just about to open it when her arm was grabbed roughly and she was spun round to find him glaring at her angrily.

'Where do you think you're going?'

'Let go of my arm, you're hurting me! I

was only going to get my things from the car!'

Laura stared up into his face in fright. All the menace of their first meeting was back in his eyes but as he took in her words she saw him relax and smile.

'I'm sorry. I'll help you unload, OK?'

'No, it's not "OK"! What did you think you were doing just now? As soon as I went to the door you leapt over and grabbed me almost as if you want to keep me prisoner here! What's the matter with you? Why can't I leave if I want to?'

She stared up at him, her green eyes glinting, but despite her anger Laura was terrified. Perhaps this man was some kind of maniac, and here she was, trapped with him in a remote cottage in the fells!

It took all her courage not to flinch when he reached forward and took both her shoulders in his powerful hands.

'Look, Laura, I'm sorry I frightened you. Of course I'm not keeping you a prisoner here. You can leave any time you want to except that it would be downright dangerous for you to do so right now.'

'What do you mean?'

He opened the door and they stood there together and looked down into the valley.

While they had been talking the snow had been falling steadily. It was already lying so thickly that there was no sign of the road. The tracks Laura had made just a short time ago were lost without trace.

It was not John Norton that was keeping her prisoner; it was the weather. They were snowed in.

TWO

The snow had insulated them from the world and here, inside the cottage, the only sound was the crackling of the log fire which sent its welcome heat into all corners of the room.

They had unloaded Laura's car, made a meal in the little kitchen and sat and eaten it together by the fire as if they had known each other all their lives.

Laura was tired. The events of the past two days were beginning to catch up with her and she knew she could very easily fall asleep if it wasn't for the questions that kept niggling away in her mind.

First of all there was the question of the fire. If John Norton had intended to stay why hadn't he made a proper fire in the first place instead of making do with the old electric fire – and why had he put it out before she arrived? Only just before she arrived, because it had still been warm.

Of course if he had left it on she would have seen the glow of the bars through the windows and she would have known that someone was in the cottage. And if he had made a proper fire there would have been smoke from the chimney – a sure sign that the cottage was inhabited.

She glanced at him as he carried the dishes through to the kitchen, and then she heard the tap running as he filled the kettle.

The warmth and her fatigue were resulting in increasing drowsiness. Laura frowned as she tried to concentrate on the things that were worrying her.

His explanation for half strangling her the minute she arrived had seemed reasonable at the time. As they'd shared their meal companionably, sitting on the sofa with plates balanced on their knees, he'd told her that, wearing jeans and muffled up as she had been against the weather, he had no idea that she was female and had imagined that she was one of the young thugs who break into empty holiday cottages and vandalize them.

But the more she thought about it, the less sense it made. Even if he had really believed that, there would have been no need for such violence. John Norton was more than a match for any man, never mind a young thug. He could simply have faced any intruder and asked for an explanation rather than resort to concealment and violence – unless he had something to fear...

Then he had said that he was simply a walker who had been caught out by the change in the weather. Was it just coincidence that he had been near to the only cottage for miles that he had believed would be empty?

It was almost as if he had planned to stay here. And another thing, how had he got in? Why hadn't she thought of that before!

Suddenly she was completely awake and on her feet, her eyes wide open as he came back through the kitchen door carrying mugs of tea.

The smile froze on his face. 'What is it? Why are you staring at me like that?'

'How did you get in here? There's no sign of a break-in – have you got a key?'

His features relaxed. 'Is that all that's worrying you? Here, come with me.'

He put the hot drinks down on a small table near the fireplace, took her by the hand and led her into the kitchen. He stood her by the sink and went out of the back door, closing it after himself.

Above the wooden bench there was an old sash window. A small sneck on the top of the bottom half was all that kept the window closed.

As Laura watched she saw this sneck moving and, finally, slipping free from its catch. Then the bottom half of the window was raised and John Norton climbed in on to the kitchen bench. In his hand he held a penknife; the blade was slim enough to slide between the two halves of the window and that was how he had opened the catch.

'That's a trick I learned when I was at boarding-school – useful when you're coming back late after lights out!'

He was smiling but Laura didn't respond. He went on, 'Look, I'm sorry if I've worried you by showing you how easy it is to break into your property. The minute this is all over you can buy some safety locks – so I've done you a favour, really, haven't I?'

It sounded plausible, but Laura was still uneasy. The cold from the stone floor began to penetrate the soles of the old slippers she was wearing and she was suddenly overcome with fatigue. She sighed wearily.

'Come back to the fire, Laura, and have your drink before it gets cold.'

She allowed herself to be led back into the living-room and she sat down by the fire once more.

'Here, drink this.'

Laura gasped after the first gulp of what she had supposed was only tea.

'There's something in that to take the chill off!'

He smiled and she began to relax. She was too tired to worry about anything more today. She closed her eyes and lay back.

John Norton crossed to the door where the light switch was, put it out and went back to sit beside her. It was early afternoon but the day was already dark and now they sat together in the firelight.

She must have dozed for a while for when she woke up she was disorientated. Her fuddled brain made her think she was back in her flat.

Despite the warmth from the fire she felt cold as she remembered everything that had happened there. The shame that Maxine's accusations had brought and the anguish at the way Steve had deserted her. She still could not believe how easily taken in she had been.

She was brought back to the present with a shock when she heard John Norton's voice.

'You know, Laura, you haven't told me why you're here.'

His question angered her. 'I don't have to tell you why I'm here – this is my cottage and I can come any time I want to!'

She stared at him defiantly, completely unaware of how appealing she looked.

He remained calm. 'I know that, but why now? Why come on your own, in winter, in these conditions? You must have had a very powerful reason!'

Suddenly she began to cry. She turned her face away so that he should not see the tears.

He stared at her and saw a child. He guessed she was not much more than twenty but, right now, she looked hardly much older than his daughter, whom he had seen sobbing in anguish only two nights before. Stifling his own pain, he reached out and took her in his arms.

Laura stiffened momentarily and then she relaxed. No one had comforted her like this for a long time. She had no close relatives and she had been alone in the world since her parents had died, the victims of a terrorists' bomb.

The unexpected tenderness released all her pent-up emotion. Laura found herself sobbing her heart out in the arms of a complete stranger.

The last thing he needed was a weeping female, and yet he found himself stroking her hair and murmuring words of comfort as he held her close against the warmth of his body.

She had not told him but he imagined that it had been the painful ending of some boy-girl romance that had brought her here to seek refuge in the cottage. Orphaned, as he knew she was, there must have been no one to turn to. Probably, no one even knew she was here. He would have to make sure of that in the morning – or at least before the thaw set in.

The snow had given him a breathing space. They were alone in the cottage in this high valley, cut off from the world. He was safe for the moment.

The sobbing had stopped and, from the change in the pattern of her breathing, he realized that she was sleeping once more. All expression left his face and he stared into the flames.

Now that he could relax, his own weariness engulfed him. Soon, with the unforeseen, sweet warmth of the girl in his arms, his eyes closed. The man and Laura slept together in the firelight.

As the hours passed, the snow stopped falling and the moon, emerging from behind the clouds, shone with a cold, hard light. A million frosty stars sparkled in the black sky. The valley looked like a scene from a Christmas card.

A light wind sprang up and sent flurries of loose snow chasing along the tops of the old stone walls. Drifts had formed against the sides of the cottage.

Inside, the fire burned low and the man stirred in his sleep. The slight movement disturbed Laura and she turned in his arms to rest her face against his body.

It was a long time since he had held a woman like this and, in his half waking, half sleeping state, desire rose unbidden. Hardly knowing what he did, his lips sought hers.

Laura sighed and turned her face away. The man came fully awake to find he was kissing the fragrant hollow of her neck.

Laura moaned softly. Her arms went around him and she clung to him with an answering desire.

'Steve,' she whispered. 'Oh, Steve…'

He stopped immediately and, taking her shoulders, he eased her back against the cushions. Gently sliding off the sofa to kneel on the floor, he lifted her feet up and covered her with the tartan rug which had been draped across the back of one of the armchairs.

He stood and looked down at the sleeping girl. The glow from the fire warmed her creamy skin and picked out the highlights in her rich, copper-coloured hair.

Even in sleep she looked sad, and he wondered what kind of an argument she could have had with the boy, whose name she had called out, to make her run away like this. He hoped, when it was all over, she would find happiness again.

He smiled, grimly, when he remembered his own reaction to having her in his arms. He did not blame himself – but he was surprised that it could have happened. He'd been sure that recent events in his own life had sickened him of love and desire forever.

But, after all, he was a normal man. He would have to be careful – there was no telling how long they would have to remain alone here together and there was no place in his plans for any kind of involvement.

Abruptly, he turned and knelt to restore the fire. He built it up with the last of the logs from the basket, then went into the kitchen and shut the door behind him.

The logs crackled and shifted in the flames.

Outside the wind grew stronger and blew a flurry of snow across the roof of the cottage. Some of it came straight down the chimney and landed in the fire with a spurt and a sizzle which sent sparks out on to the stone hearth. They lay there, flared up for a moment and then died, but the noise had woken Laura.

The first thing she noticed was the warmth. Laura smiled and stretched luxuriously and, as she did so, she dislodged the rug and it fell on to the floor.

Then, as she bent to retrieve it, she remembered her situation. She had fled to her cottage because Steve had left her to run after his wife. The wife that Laura never knew he had.

She sat curled up on the sofa and pulled the rug around her as it all came back. She was alone with a complete stranger, who sometimes acted like a madman, and it looked as though she might have to stay here with him until the thaw.

Laura glanced over towards the kitchen door and she saw a thin line of light along the bottom. She could hear him moving around, filling a kettle, setting out cups.

She had counted on being alone here. She needed time to sort out her feelings and overcome her heartbreak.

Laura wrapped her arms around her legs and rested her chin on her knees. She stared pensively into the flames. Was she heartbroken? To have your heart broken you had to be in love, didn't you, and, to be honest, she had never been absolutely sure whether the feeling she had for Steve was love. Certainly he had made her happy.

He had breezed into her life and forced her to come out of the shell she had built around herself since her parents had died. He had shown her how to laugh again. Even the quality of her work improved after she met Steve – he had the ability to make you believe that all things were possible. She had grown to need him.

And he had made her believe that he needed her just as much. He needed the peace and tranquillity of their time together in the riverside apartment. He needed her innocence and to be able to look at life anew through her young eyes.

He said that underneath his outward show of easy going camaraderie he was just as lonely as she was – that he had never had anyone to share his hopes and dreams with – but it had all been lies!

Laura gasped in pain as she realized she

had bitten into her lower lip with her top teeth. A drop of blood began to trickle down her chin. She had no handkerchief or tissues handy so she tried to stop the flow with her hand.

It was no good, she would have to go into the kitchen and grab a paper towel. If she kept her head down she could pretend she'd had a nose bleed – she didn't want John Norton to guess how strong her emotions were and what they had made her do. It would be too embarrassing.

Laura opened the door but then stared round in surprise. The kitchen was empty! But how could it be? Just a few moments ago she thought she had heard him moving around in here. Could it be that he had decided to leave without telling her?

Or perhaps he didn't even exist – perhaps her lack of sleep and state of confusion had made her imagine the whole incident. How wonderful if she had the cottage to herself after all!

But then a slight hissing sound made her look over to the stove. The kettle was beginning to boil and there were two mugs set out on the bench next to a jar of instant coffee and a box of teabags.

So she hadn't imagined the sounds she

had heard. Her unwelcome guest was real and he must have left the kitchen only moments ago.

At that moment the door opened forcefully and John Norton backed into the room in a swirl of snowflakes. He turned and kicked the door shut behind him. In his arms he carried a large cardboard box full of logs.

He didn't see Laura because he was wearing a parka with the hood pulled well forward over his face and he was looking down at the logs he carried.

It wasn't until he had eased his load down onto the floor and straightened up that he noticed her.

'My God, what have you done to your face?'

Laura became conscious of the trickle of blood on her chin and neck.

'N-nothing – I – I must have bitten my lip in my sleep,' she faltered, but he didn't pause to question her.

'Here, let me have a look.'

He pulled off his gloves and took her face firmly in one large hand. It was surprising how gentle he was. He turned her face towards the light bulb hanging in the centre of the room and examined it carefully.

'You'll live – it's just a small wound, but

you'd better wash it with some antiseptic. I've got a first-aid kit in my rucksack.'

'Thanks, but I've got some stuff in the kitchen cupboard. My parents always insisted on keeping the cottage ship-shape and ready for the next visit.'

Laura busied herself cleaning up her face. She filled a small bowl with boiling water from the kettle and, whilst it cooled, got out a bottle of antiseptic and some cotton wool.

When she had finished she turned to find him smiling at her. 'Mmm, you smell delicious, just like a nurse I once knew. No matter how many showers she took, she always arrived for our dates smelling antiseptic and germfree!'

Laura laughed uncertainly. This was the first time he had spoken to her without seeming to weigh up every word and the effect it might have. He had let his guard down and she had a glimpse of the kind of man he must be if only...

Laura frowned. If only what? If only he weren't the kind of man who had to take refuge in a lonely cottage in the fells? If only he didn't have to be suspicious of anyone who approached him?

She closed her eyes momentarily. She had no idea where her thoughts were leading her. When she opened them again and looked up the smile had gone. He was staring at her intently again as if he were trying to read her mind.

He began to take off the parka and when he hung it on the back of the door, Laura realized it was her father's. As he kicked off her father's wellingtons he saw her stricken expression and guessed the reason.

He said gently, 'He wouldn't have minded, Laura. He'd have been pleased that when they were needed they were here – and that they were the right size!'

Laura knew he spoke the truth. She had a sudden insight that the two men would have got on very well – her father and John Norton.

She reached forward for the kettle. 'Do you want tea or coffee?'

'Tea, please, and when you've made it, put the kettle on again. There's still a long way to go before dawn and I think the best place for you is upstairs in bed, so you'd better fill up some hot-water bottles – I noticed you've got some hanging on the back of the pantry door.'

They drank their tea by the fire. She had brought some chocolate digestive biscuits and she opened the packet and shook some out on to a plate. She offered them to her companion and then, as she ate her own, she put the plate down on the hearth. A moment later she had to move it. The heat from the fire was so intense that the chocolate coating had begun to melt.

The warmth was beginning to permeate the whole house so it wasn't as bad as she thought it was going to be when she went upstairs. She had slept in this room since she was a child and it was still decorated with the Laura Ashley wallpaper she and her mother had chosen together when she was fourteen.

Before she closed the curtains she stood and looked out at the snow-filled valley. The snow, sparkling with pinpoints of frost in the moonlight, looked so beautiful against the backdrop of the diamond-encrusted sky that it was easy to forget the danger of her situation.

She got clean sheets from the linen cupboard on the tiny landing. The hot-water tank, heated from the fire's back boiler, had made the cupboard warm and cosy so that the sheets already had the chill taken off.

He brought up the hot-water bottles just as she was smoothing down the quilted eiderdown and he put them all in her bed.

'But what about you? Don't you want any?'

'I shan't need them. I shall be sleeping downstairs by the fire.'

'But it's all right – I mean, I don't mind if you sleep in my parents' bed. Just as you said before, they would have been glad it was there when it was needed.'

'Thank you, but one of us should be downstairs to make sure the fire doesn't go out. You're very tired and you must sleep without interruption for as long as you need. Now, no objections, good-night and sleep well!'

As he settled his large frame on the sofa the man grimaced cynically. Oh, it was true enough that he wanted to tend the fire but, it was also true that he thought it much wiser to sleep downstairs rather than just across the landing from Laura Stewart.

What on earth had come over him? In the kitchen just a short while ago, he had wanted to take her in his arms and kiss her poor lip better!

He must not allow himself to get close to her. He needed all his wits about him if he was going to come through his present troubles unscathed.

Their situation, thrown together in adverse

41

conditions and cut off from the world by the snow, was creating a false sense of closeness and security. He must never forget that, when the snow melted, his sanctuary would cease to exist.

But now he could be thankful for what he had. A warm and comfortable place to shelter for one night at least. Wearily, he closed his eyes. The tensions and the terrors of the last few days had drained him. He gave way to the demands of his exhausted body and his sleep was deep and dreamless.

But in the little room upstairs Laura was wide awake.

THREE

The winter night pressed down on the cottage and Laura lay, curled up tight under the bedclothes, not daring to examine the awful suspicion that had been growing steadily in her mind.

When she had taken flight from an emotional situation that she couldn't handle, to hide out in her childhood home, she had not foreseen that a sudden worsening of the weather would cut off her retreat and leave her stranded in the high fells with a murderer.

There, she had admitted it to herself. The man who had taken possession of her cottage was not who he claimed to be. He was not John Norton, a stranded fell walker. He must have invented that name for himself on the spur of the moment when he saw Laura's eyes stray to the metal initials punched into his rucksack.

They were his initials, all right, but the J.N stood for Julian North, the man wanted for the brutal slaying of his wife. Laura was sure of it.

Cautiously, she sat up a little and raised her head. The room was warm enough, now, but she shivered as she strained to listen for any sounds that might tell her if the man downstairs was asleep or awake.

She could hear nothing. He must be sleeping on the sofa in front of the fire as he had intended.

She reached out and switched on the bedside lamp, then she pushed down the bedclothes and swung her legs over the side of the bed. She paused before she put her feet on the floor. She had remembered the squeaky floor-board. She would have to trust that her memory of its position was accurate and tiptoe around it.

Moments later, her heart thudding painfully, she was standing in front of the cupboard in the niche beside the chimney breast.

The door opened easily. Inside, her old toys and books were stacked neatly on the shelves as though they had only been put aside the day before. Laura reached into a cardboard box and found what she was looking for: a transistor radio. She had left it there last time she had been at the cottage.

Once back in bed she put the radio on the

small table beside the lamp and switched it on.

A burst of static followed by pop music made Laura grab the radio hastily and pull it under the blankets. She covered her head and eased down inside the bed a little, then she adjusted the volume.

She hoped that the sudden sound had not alerted the man downstairs. She did not want him to know that she was awake and waiting for a news bulletin on the radio.

When it came, Laura discovered that the 'Belgravia murder' was still making the headlines. She listened intently. First of all, the newsreader updated the listener on the known facts.

Geraldine North had been savagely beaten to death in her luxury apartment. Her husband, journalist Julian North, was known to have returned to England that night from an assignment abroad and there was good reason to believe that he had been in the house. He had, however, disappeared and the police were very anxious to discover his whereabouts.

Laura tensed instinctively. If only she could tell them!

The newsreader had paused slightly and now went on to impart some new facts.

Apparently it had only just been revealed that the Norths' seven-year-old daughter, Sally, was thought to have been in the house with her mother but there was no sign of her. The police were very anxious to trace her and were concerned for her safety.

There was no more about the Belgravia case and Laura switched off the radio. She was bewildered.

If John Norton was Julian North then where was Sally, his daughter? Laura could imagine circumstances in which a man might murder his wife but what kind of monster would dispose of a child? If her theory was correct he must have done so, for there was certainly no sign of Sally North in the cottage.

Laura went over it all in her mind. She had never really believed the man's story about being innocently caught out by the weather. Parts of the set-up had not rung true: little things, like not betraying his presence in the cottage by lighting a fire, and much more sinister things, like the way he had jumped on her and almost throttled her the moment she set foot in the place.

Laura wondered, now, how he had managed to talk her round.

She tried very hard to imagine what his

face would be like without the abundant growth of black hair. The very beard which gave him the rugged, outdoor look of a genuine fell walker was also an excellent disguise.

She had seen Julian North on television and she tried the process in reverse – adding a beard to the image she remembered. She frowned – it could be the same face but she could not swear to it.

It was a while since she had seen him. Now she thought about it, she realized that he had been off the screen for at least a year although he had continued to write articles for the quality press and she had heard his radio reports from South East Asia.

That was probably where he had grown the beard. On television, beards, while not forbidden, are not encouraged, but on the radio, it just doesn't matter. She wondered if he had grown it because he needed a disguise while working on an investigative story. If so, it was also proving to be very useful now!

Then Laura's eyes widened and suddenly she grew very still. She had just realized why she had been so convinced that she recognized him – it was his distinctive voice. Although she could not be sure if that was

Julian North's face under the heavy beard, there was no disguising his voice. She remembered that she had thought it familiar from almost the first moment she had heard him speak.

She could not imagine how he had made his escape from London, why he had chosen to take refuge here in the Pennine Fells or, more worryingly, where his daughter was.

She only knew that she must go immediately. She must leave the cottage whilst he was sleeping and somehow, make her way to the nearest village and raise the alarm.

Laura crept over to the window and looked out across the countryside. She shivered. The first thing she must do would be to dress warmly and with the weather in mind. Luckily she had brought her things upstairs.

Laura frowned. She seemed to remember that she had left her boots and anorak by the door but that should not prove too much of a problem if she could grab them quickly.

Once she was dressed she looked out of the window again. Half-way down the fellside there was an old wood. In happier times Laura would often leave the track and cut down through the trees which reached right down to the road which led into the village.

She was sure that she would remember the way. The biggest problem would be crossing the open expanse of snow-covered fells in the bright moonlight. But there was no alternative – she would have to take the risk.

The stairs led straight into the sitting-room. The light was out and Laura could see the man lying on the sofa by the fire. His deep and regular breathing told her that he was fast asleep.

Laura paused in the shadows. She could see her anorak hanging by the door and her boots on the floor below.

The last few steps down seemed to take forever. Reaching up for her anorak and stooping swiftly to gather up her boots were the bravest things Laura had ever done.

Trembling, she opened the door and slid out into the night, pulling it closed behind her as fast as she could in case an inrush of cold air awakened the man by the fire.

There was no shout of alarm. No heavy footsteps pounding towards the door. Pulling on her boots and anorak as quickly as she could and fishing her hat out of a pocket and pulling it on her head, she set off across the snow at a run.

It was heavy going, running through the snow and she was soon out of breath but there were no signs of pursuit and, after a while, Laura realized that she was safe. She had made good her escape. Her spirits lifted as she drew nearer to the trees and then something made her stop and look back at the cottage. It looked so peaceful in the moonlight.

Laura found that there were tears in her eyes. She shook her head angrily. Were those tears for her lost childhood and those happy days spent in the cottage with her parents or were they for something much more recent?

She clenched her fists. The man was a murderer. He had killed his wife and maybe even his daughter, too. So w........s she crying for him?

And why had that scene come leaping unbidden to her mind the moment she had turned to look at the cottage? Laura turned away and tried to suppress the picture that was tormenting her. The picture of the man and the girl sleeping in each other's arms beside the fire. She set off once more towards the woods.

The tangled branches of the trees assumed fantastic shapes against the night sky. If Laura had not known the path so well she would have been fearful to step out of the bright moonlight into the eerie shadowland of the winter woods. But how much more fearful was the alternative? No, she must go on.

There were places under the thick shelter of the branches that the snow had not reached. The dead leaves crackled underfoot and there was no hope of Laura moving quietly along the winding paths. Still, she thought, there was no one to hear her. No one but the startled wildlife. Laura had no idea what creatures she disturbed in her flight but she could hear their anxious movements and chatterings as she went by.

She had started off confidently, convinced that she would remember the path she used to take when she was a child. But Laura had never been in the woods at night-time and it did not take her long to discover how fearsomely different the familiar paths looked after dark. Soon she realized that she was lost.

The sound of a fallen branch breaking under her foot startled her. She stopped and listened but there was no sign that she was being followed. Laura was now so deep into the woods that she did not even know if it would be quicker to try to retrace her steps or go on. As the stillness closed in on her once more, and her heart stopped pounding, she smiled wryly. She was no longer very sure which was the way forward or which the way back.

And then a glint of something bright drew her attention. Laura grasped the tree trunk nearest to her and stared intently between the twisted shapes of the trees.

She saw the moon shining on a stretch of water and remembered that there was a small lake not far from the road. She was going the right way!

Laura breathed a sigh of relief and plunged forward through the brushwood, taking the short cut to the lake shore. That was her undoing.

Before she realized what had happened she had stumbled headlong into a tangle of thorn bushes and, as she fought to free herself from the sharp-toothed stems, she lost her balance and came crashing down.

Laura flung up her arms to protect her face from the thorns but this made her fall awkwardly and her right leg twisted under her. The resulting pain was agonizing. She could not stop herself from crying out.

She crouched in the undergrowth, listening intently, in case anyone had heard her. She did not know how long she stayed there, growing colder by the minute. She listened to the rustling noises made by spiders hunting through the dead leaves. The sudden scream of a vixen calling out to its mate filled the wood with unearthly echoes. Laura shivered instinctively but the only sounds she could hear were the normal night sounds of the winter countryside.

She breathed a sigh of relief and began to get up. Immediately, a stab of pain in her right ankle brought the tears to her eyes. She stood clinging on to a tree trunk while she tested putting the weight on her right foot. She couldn't do it.

Whether she had broken her ankle or merely sprained it badly, she was temporarily crippled. The only way she could go on to the village would be to crawl.

Laura closed her eyes. She would rest for a while but before her body temperature dropped too much she would get down on all fours and continue on her way. She was in no position to give up now!

The months since her parents had died had taught her much. She had had to learn to survive on her own. But at least the money they had left had provided financial security. Laura had been studying Art and Design at the Newcastle College and she had already had some success with her designs for jewellery. As soon as she had finished her course she had been able to move out of the students' hostel, buy her riverside apartment and concentrate on her career. She was elated to be taken on by Chris Martin at the developing Blackfriars Craft Centre.

But, no matter how well her professional life had developed, she had been very lonely. Her friends from college had seemed embarrassed by her tragedy and, although they had been kind at first, as soon as they saw that she was coping, they returned to their own busy lives.

She had worked hard and become more and more isolated. Until she met Steve.

Laura clutched at the rough bark of the tree trunk. She did not want to remember that particular problem now. She had plenty more to worry about.

Suddenly she noticed that the quality of the night sounds had changed. Amongst the normal rustlings and murmurings of the wood at night-time she imagined she could hear something else.

The snapping of a twig, low branches of brushwood swishing as something big moved stealthily along the narrow paths. The sounds were coming nearer. She opened her eyes in alarm and stared round wildly. Julian North was heading straight towards her.

Laura stirred and moved cautiously as her unwilling senses returned. Where was she?

She felt warm. But how could that be? She remembered crouching on the cold woodland floor – no, she had been supporting herself by hanging on to a tree. But why had she been in the woods at night?

She had been escaping, that was it. Running away from the cottage because–

She opened her eyes wide in alarm as memory came flooding back. She was back in the cottage, on the sofa by the fire and Julian North was standing over her!

Laura screamed.

Swiftly the man bent down and grasped her shoulders. Laura went rigid with fright but she managed to gasp out, 'Let go of me!'

'I will if you promise not to scream again.'

'Why bother about that? There's no one near enough to hear me!'

In spite of her terror, Laura felt her courage returning. She knew there was nothing to stop him adding her to his list of victims, but at least she wouldn't go without a fight!

'That's not what's bothering me, Laura.

It's just that you made such a dreadful noise!'

He was actually smiling!

The man did let go of her shoulders but he knelt down and stared at her intently.

'And besides, I don't want you getting upset. Perhaps you don't remember but when I found you in the woods you tried to run and then you screamed in pain before you fainted. You seemed to have damaged one of your ankles. I had to carry you back. I think you should try to relax, now.'

Relax, when she was sharing her cottage with a murderer! Laura smothered a desire to laugh hysterically.

'Why did you run away, Laura?'

Laura thought he must be mad to ask that question, but then she remembered that he did not know that she had been listening to the radio. He did not know that she knew about the 'Belgravia murder' or that she suspected he was the wanted man. There was just the chance that he might still think that she believed his cover story. She would have to act as if that were true. The stakes were high and it was worth a try.

'I wanted to telephone–'

He was alert instantly. 'Telephone who?'

'Let me finish! I wanted to telephone Steve

– my b-boyfriend. I quarrelled with him and I ran away– I – I wanted to say sorry…'

Laura trailed off. He was staring at her coldly and she forced herself to return his gaze.

'You wanted to say sorry in the middle of the night?'

'Why not? He's probably worrying about me.'

'But to go out in these conditions – possibly risk your life?'

'Have you never been in love?'

Laura watched him as he considered her and she saw the moment when his shoulders relaxed almost imperceptibly. Incredible as it might seem, she thought he believed her. Laura found she had been holding her breath and she let it out with a shaky sigh.

'Yes, I've been in love, Laura. I know what terrible things love can make you do.'

His voice was cold and Laura shivered. She did not want to dwell on the implication of his words. He was still staring at her.

'But why did you go without telling me?'

'I thought you would stop me.'

She forced herself to remain calm and not to betray her relief when he smiled.

'You're right, of course. I would have

stopped you. It was madness to go out there alone – especially to go the way you did. I could hardly believe it when I followed your tracks and I saw that they led straight into the woods.'

'Why did you follow me?'

The man stared at her thoughtfully and Laura wished she had not asked that question but he merely shrugged.

'It's just as well that I did. You wouldn't have got much further with that damaged ankle. If I hadn't woken up and found you gone you might have frozen to death before morning.'

Laura thought it best not to ask what had made him go upstairs to check her bedroom. She already knew the answer and it was much safer if she did not force him to admit that he was worried that she knew too much.

'Ouch! What are you doing? Let go of me!'

'Relax, Laura. I only want to examine your ankle – I think it's sprained, not broken, but I'd better strap it up for you. Can you wriggle out of your jeans while I get a bandage from the first-aid kit?'

Laura thought of protesting but decided not to. Her ankle was painful and she might as well let him help her.

By the time he came back from the kitchen she had taken off her jeans and tights and wrapped the rug around herself. She stretched her leg out on the sofa in front of her.

He was both gentle and skilful and caused her as little pain as possible. When he had finished he went back into the kitchen to boil the kettle. Soon he returned with a tray containing a mug of tea each, some biscuits and a couple of painkillers.

'These should dull the pain. They're very good – I always carry them when I'm away from home working on – when I'm away from home.'

Laura took the tablets and smiled to herself. What had he been going to say? 'Working on an assignment?' Perhaps his guard was beginning to slip. He had almost revealed something about his personal life.

Another winter dawn lightened the windows as they sat together by the fire once more. It seemed to Laura that the days were beginning to run in to each other. She began to feel drowsy.

She stared into the fire. The flames crackled and leapt in the hearth cheerily. Laura smiled slowly as she remembered sitting here as a child and imagining pictures in the fire.

She yawned.

The pain in her ankle had receded and she began to relax. Her head felt light and yet strangely heavy as it dropped back into the cushions on the sofa. She felt so strange. So light and peaceful – she would just lie here for a while. Just lie and watch the pretty flames until she went to sleep...

The man moved forward to put another log on the fire and the bulk of his body became a menacing silhouette as, momentarily, it shut out the light and the warmth. Laura shivered. Then she frowned as somewhere in her fuddled brain fear stirred. She opened her eyes wide. Something was wrong.

The tablets! What were those tablets he had given her?

Frantically she fought to sit up but her limbs were as heavy as lead. She tried to cry out but only managed a soft moan.

The man turned to look at her. He saw the panic in her face and intuitively guessed its cause. He took hold of her shoulders gently.

'Don't worry, the tablets won't harm you. They'll only make you sleep for a while. Trust me.'

Laura stared up into his eyes. Her own eyes were closing but, before they did, she had to see if she could believe him. He held her gaze without flinching. He was still looking at her when sleep overcame her.

FOUR

When Laura woke up she could hear talking. Or rather, she could hear a woman's voice, low and persistent. She stretched and frowned. As memory came back she realized that this was impossible and she sat up quickly.

The voice had stopped. Had she imagined it or had it been part of her muddled dreams? Like most dreams they were fading fast as she awakened, but Laura seemed to remember Maxine had figured in them and they had not been pleasant.

She sighed and the sigh turned into a groan. In spite of the dreams, she felt rested and strangely at ease. She could remember every detail of her situation and yet she could not bring herself to worry about it. Perhaps it was something to do with the tablets she had taken or perhaps it was simply because she was young and resilient, but she did not feel afraid.

Sunlight flooded in across the little downstairs room of the cottage and the fire crackled in the hearth.

There was something else. Laura realized that the most delicious smells of frying bacon were coming from the kitchen. At that moment the door opened and John Norton came in carrying a tray.

Laura saw that he had pulled the table into the sunlight by the window and it was already set up with cutlery, crocks and a steaming pot of tea. He smiled when he saw that she was awake.

'It's a little late for breakfast, so we'll call it brunch. Just wait a moment and I'll help you over to the table.'

As he placed the plates of bacon, eggs and fried bread down onto the red and white gingham cloth, Laura wriggled into her jeans under the cover of the blanket.

When John Norton helped her to her feet her ankle only gave a slight twinge of pain but she realized that she would not be able to put too much weight on it for a day or two.

The meal was delicious and Laura discovered that she was hungry. It wasn't until she had finished her fourth slice of toast and marmalade that she realized that the man had placed their chairs in such a way that she had to squint into direct sunlight if she wanted to look at his face.

She guessed that this would not have been accidental and she grimaced wryly.

'What's the matter? Don't you like my cooking?'

'Your cooking is first rate, I was just – just thinking...'

Laura trailed off unhappily. She did not want to risk angering him by telling him the exact nature of her thoughts. But he didn't question her. He was busy pouring them each another cup of tea. While he did so, Laura turned to look out of the window.

The valley was beautiful with the sun shining on the snow, but the air looked clear and cold. Laura guessed there had been very little thaw.

The man was watching her. Once more, he seemed to have read her thoughts.

'You and I will have to put up with one another's company for a while longer, Laura.'

Laura spoke impulsively. 'I don't see why.'

'What do you mean?'

'It's not actually snowing. There are still some hours of daylight – we could easily get to the village if we wanted to.'

'Why should we want to? We have plenty of food and logs for the fire. We're warm and

65

safe. Why should we risk going out? After all, neither of us has anywhere special to go – do we?'

Laura felt the underlying tension. She knew she ought to drop the subject but something forced her to go on.

'Well, I don't know about you but I'd very much like to get to a phone box–'

He was sitting very still. She sensed that he was listening intently for her next words.

'–and phone Steve,' she finished.

She felt uncomfortable using Steve as an excuse. In reality, she never wanted to speak to Steve Fraser again but the man was not to know that.

'Oh, yes, the boyfriend. Well whatever it is that you two have quarrelled about he'll just have to suffer for a little longer. It would be very unwise of you to set off for the village on your own and I'm certainly not taking you.'

'That's not fair. Poor Steve will be very worried!'

'Why?'

'After our quarrel I just packed up and left – he doesn't even know where I am and there's no way he can find out unless I phone him!'

'I see.'

The moment the words had left her mouth Laura knew what a mistake she had made. Her attempt at a cover story had only revealed that no one knew where she was so no one would come here looking for her. She was completely at his mercy.

He had got up from the table and was acting as if nothing significant had been said.

'It's getting a little chilly sitting here by the window – let's finish our tea near the fire.'

He carried the cups across the room and placed them down on the hearth and then he returned to help Laura. She had forgotten about her ankle and when she got up she cried out as the pain struck and she stumbled into his arms.

'Are you ok?'

'Yes – I–'

Laura broke off as she felt tears pricking at the back of her eyes. A moment later they had welled up and were spilling down her cheeks. She found herself sobbing helplessly.

'Don't worry, Laura.'

Gently the man pulled her into his arms. 'Cry if you want to.'

'I d-don't usually burst into tears s-so frequently – I d-don't understand–'

'It's only delayed shock. You've been

through quite a lot in the last few days. There, there, my dear, don't worry about it – just lean on me – I don't mind.'

They stood there in the middle of the small living-room of the cottage. The weak sunlight fell across her copper-coloured hair and, without realizing what he was doing, he began to brush it back from her tearstained face. He held her tightly against his body and he could feel the moment when her sobs began to subside. He put one hand gently under her chin and raised her face towards his. She looked up at him with candid, sea-green eyes.

Laura felt his sudden intake of breath and then his mouth came down on hers. At first the kiss was gentle, questioning, but as he felt her awakening response, he became more demanding until they clung to each other for dear life. Time and place were forgotten as they discovered a mounting and mutual joy.

Then suddenly he tore himself away from her and she felt bereft.

'I'm sorry, Laura – that was unforgivable.'

In one swift movement he lifted her up into his arms and placed her on the sofa by the fire. 'That tea will be cold. I'll make some more – we both need it.'

He was gone. Laura heard him filling the kettle in the kitchen. She curled up in the corner of the sofa and gazed into the fire. She thought about what had just occurred. There was no denying her response to his kisses and her overwhelming delight. Nothing that had ever happened between her and Steve had come anywhere near such a dizzying loss of control. If John Norton had not broken away from her Laura doubted if she would have been able to deny him anything. Then, as her senses returned to normal, a sense of shock took over. What kind of person was she, who could respond like that to a man who was probably a murderer?

When he came back with the tea she found that she could not look him in the face.

'I need the bathroom – I don't think I can manage the stairs just yet – I'll just go through to the little cloakroom at the back. It's all right – I don't need help.'

Laura clutched the furniture as she stumbled through to the kitchen. It was true, she did need the bathroom but she also needed some time to compose herself.

Her father had converted a small store-room at the back of the cottage into a tiny cloakroom with a lavatory, washbasin and shower cubicle. After Laura had made herself comfortable she splashed cold water on her burning face and dragged a comb through her tangled curls. Then she felt ready to go back and face him.

He had made up the fire and was staring into the flames moodily, pretty much as Laura had been doing just a short while ago. She wondered what he was thinking. When he saw that she had come back into the room he turned and made the effort to smile. 'Come and drink your tea.'

Laura settled herself on the sofa as far away from him as she could and he laughed. 'Don't worry, I'm not going to molest you. I really am sorry for what happened just now – let's just put it down to propinquity.'

Laura felt strangely let down. She had never responded like that to anyone and yet, the man was more or less saying that it had only happened because they were alone together in the confined space of the cottage. She did not want this to be true – and yet the real reason it had happened was even worse. She sighed and sipped her tea.

'Do you want to tell me why you ran away? What poor Steve did that made you take such drastic action?'

Laura glared at him. 'Why do you want to know?'

'Don't be so suspicious. I just thought it might help you to talk about it.'

'Well it won't. And, anyway, I don't wish to discuss my private life with you any more than I imagine you would be willing to tell me the real reason why you are here!'

Laura gasped as she realized what she had said but she forced herself to meet his gaze. He looked at her long and levelly and, finally, it was the man who turned away. 'I wish you hadn't said that.'

In spite of the warmth from the fire Laura felt cold.

After a while he turned to face her and Laura could have sworn that his smile was tinged with regret. But all he said was, 'I think you should go upstairs and rest. I'll see to the dishes and get some kind of meal going for later on. There's plenty of hot water – you could have a bath if you like.'

Laura looked at him. It was strange – she ought to be frightened of him. Her brain was telling her that he was dangerous – that she was in peril – and yet her body did not shrink from his touch.

He was a powerful man. She would not stand a chance of defending herself if he

71

decided to do away with her. Laura sighed. There was no point in worrying.

'OK, a bath might be a good idea.' She allowed him to help her upstairs.

The bathroom was straight ahead. Laura's parents had converted a tiny, third bedroom. Originally the cottage had not had a bathroom and Laura could remember their first few holidays there when they had had to drag an old tin bath in front of the fire. She remembered what fun bath times were in those early days. Her mother would dry her in front of the fire and put on her nightdress and dressing-gown while her father made the supper.

Whenever he cooked he seemed to be inspired to sing songs from Italian operas and Laura and her mother would giggle helplessly at the sight of him waving the cooking utensils about as he acted out the part of the hero or the villain.

After supper she was allowed to curl up in one of the old armchairs by the fire. They never had a television set at the cottage and she could remember falling asleep to the sound of the classical music programmes her parents liked to listen to on the radio. Her father would carry her upstairs when they went to bed.

John Norton put her down at the head of the stairs and went ahead of her into the bathroom.

'I'll have a quick wash and brush up first, if you don't mind.'

'That's OK – I'll wait in my bedroom.'

But Laura did not go straight into her own room. Instead she pushed open the door at the other side of the tiny landing. The door that led into her parents' room.

The room looked as it always had. Tidy but in waiting. The bed was covered with a patchwork quilt, there was a jug of dried flowers on the old dresser and her father's antique carafe and drinking glasses were still on the silver tray on the bedside table.

On the table on her mother's side there was a pile of paperback crime books. Her mother loved detective stories and she had become increasingly adept at solving the mystery before she was half-way through the book. Laura's father had said she ought to be writing them herself. For relaxation he liked a good thriller – clever stuff with spies and lots of action.

Laura wondered what her parents would have made of the situation in which she now found herself. It was like one of their beloved works of fiction come true. She knew her father would have wanted her to be brave and her mother would have wanted her to keep her wits about her. Well, she would try not to let them down.

'Laura? Are you in there?'

John Norton had to stoop to enter the room, just as her father had had to.

'I was sorry to hear about your parents, Laura. I saw the press coverage at the time. I suppose your father, being a professional soldier, knew what the score was but he would never have imagined that there would be an attack on married quarters at the base.'

'At least they were together when they died.'

Laura found that she could speak about it quite calmly now. Terrorist attacks on 'soft targets' had become more commonplace since her parents had died. At the time the whole civilized world had been outraged.

'Did you ever meet my parents?'

'No, but we had mutual friends. And of course I'd covered – I mean, I knew all about your father's distinguished career. It was a matter of public record.'

What had he been going to say? That he'd covered other events in her father's active life for the media? Laura was sure that being cooped up in the snowbound cottage was beginning to have an effect on him. If what she suspected was true, he had almost let his guard slip again.

If he was worried he did not show it. 'I've finished with the bathroom. Why don't you have a good, long soak? It will do you good.'

'Right, I'll just collect some clean clothes from my room.'

As the landing was so small, the man stepped back and let Laura leave the room first. She did not look back at him but went straight ahead into her own room. When she had made her dramatic escape in the middle of the night she had not thought she would be entering it again so soon.

The blankets and eiderdown had been pulled down to the bottom of the bed as if to air the sheets. Laura knew she had not left it as tidy as this. The bedclothes had become tumbled and disarranged as she had crouched under the covers listening to the radio.

The radio was gone.

Her heart began to beat frantically as she turned swiftly to scan the bedside table.

'It's not there, Laura.'

She screamed involuntarily and looked at the doorway. He filled the whole frame, blocking any escape.

'I found the radio when I came upstairs just after you left the cottage. What had you been listening to?' Laura edged towards the bed as he came into the room.

'I w-was listening to a music programme – I couldn't sleep...' She trailed off as he came nearer.

'Was that all you were listening to?'

'Yes – what else should I listen to in the middle of the night?'

'What about the news, Laura? We both know that there are regular news bulletins on the radio.'

Laura felt sick. To her shame, her legs gave way and she found herself sinking on to the bed behind her. She tried to speak but the words stuck in her throat.

He towered above her. 'It's no use – I'd been hoping against hope that you didn't know, but I was watching you when you came into the room just now. I saw your reaction when you realized the radio had gone. You were terrified. You'd been listening to the news, hadn't you?'

'Yes,' she whispered. 'But what's w-wrong with that?'

The man sighed. 'It's no use pretending any longer. You know who I am, don't you?'

'Yes.'

He went on as if she hadn't spoken. 'As you've already guessed, I'm not John Norton. I'm Julian North, the man every police force in the British Isles is looking for. Why are you looking so frightened, Laura? Is it because you're trapped here with a murderer?'

FIVE

Laura lay back in the bath and tried not to think about what had just happened. The warm water was soothing to her aching body and she watched idly as the steam rose and curled around under the white ceiling of the tiny bathroom.

Her father had decorated the room with blush-pink tiles in deference to his women-folk and Laura had helped her mother make and hang the rose-sprigged curtains at the small, white framed window.

The curtains usually remained open as the only view from the back of the house was the steeply rising fellside. The window revealed that most of the light had gone from the sky. Another winter day was nearly over.

Laura wondered how many more she would have to spend here.

Involuntarily, she glanced over to the door. Before taking off her clothes and stepping into the bath she had turned the old-fashioned key securely in the lock – and not just out of a sense of modesty!

She sat up and pushed an escaping tendril of hair more securely into the restraining hairband and as she began to soap herself her mind returned to the scene in the bedroom.

She had sat trembling on the bed as the man loomed over her.

'Why are you looking so frightened, Laura,' he'd asked. 'Is it because you're trapped here with a murderer?'

Then to her surprise he had sunk on to his knees beside her and grasped both her hands. Her fright had made them icy-cold and he had pulled them towards his chest, holding them there, rubbing them and trying to warm them.

'Please don't be frightened, Laura,' he'd said. 'Whatever happens, I won't hurt you.'

Then Laura realized that she was not really frightened – just fearfully disturbed. She was not frightened because, for some reason, when he looked into her eyes like this, she believed him when he said he would not hurt her.

But she was disturbed at her own reaction to him. After all, he had admitted it himself, he was wanted for murder. He was suspected of killing his wife – and he had not denied the crime.

The man saw Laura's troubled frown. Once more he seemed to have read her mind. 'Don't ask me, Laura. Don't ask me any questions. Believe me, it's better if you know nothing.'

Now, lying in the bath, Laura could still not believe that she had let it go at that. She knew it wasn't fright that had kept her silent. She had simply accepted his statement – accepted that he knew best.

'Why don't you have a bath and rest for a while? I'll go downstairs and see what I can cook up for our evening meal.'

She'd sat on the bed for a moment after he had gone, and then she had hauled herself wearily into the bathroom.

She always kept the bathroom cabinet fully stocked and she'd chosen her favourite rose bath-oil to perfume the water. It was supposed to be soothing. The label said it would ease your worries clean away. Well, if it could banish her particular worries, she would write a glowing letter of commendation to the manufacturer!

As she dried herself with a giant bath towel Laura smiled to herself. At least her sense of honour seemed to be returning.

She did not hurry down. She pulled on her

old dressing-gown and tried to rest as Julian had suggested, but her mind kept returning again and again to the moment when he had knelt on the floor and sworn that he would not hurt her. She remembered her sense of loss when he had let go of her hands.

The sky was quite dark now and Laura closed the curtains and put on the bedside lamp. She tried to read one of her collection of paperbacks but found it impossible to follow the storyline when the events in her own life seemed to be more dangerous and exciting than any fiction she had ever read.

She was surprised when a glance at her watch told her that she had been upstairs for several hours. She decided it was time to go downstairs and face him.

Once dressed in a clean pair of jeans and a soft, white angora sweater, Laura paused on the landing. The most delicious smells of cooking were wafting up the stairs.

She went down slowly, one step at a time like a small child in order to avoid putting too much weight on her sprained ankle.

Julian must have heard her, for he shouted up, 'Need any help?'

'No thank you, I can manage.'

The room looked warm and inviting. While she had been upstairs he had swept the hearth and tidied up, but it was the table which drew Laura's eyes.

The sofa had been pushed back and the table pulled over nearer to the fire. It was still covered with the red-checked cloth but he had found her mother's raffia place-mats and the antique silver candlestick. The candle was red – left over from the last Christmas Laura and her parents had spent at the cottage, and around the base he had arranged some of the sweetly smelling pine cones that were kept in the drawer with the tablecloths and napkins.

Just as Laura made it to the bottom of the stairs, Julian crossed the room to switch off the light. She looked up into his face, startled, but he only grinned and reached forward to pick her up bodily.

'Here, let me carry you to the table. I don't want you stumbling in the dark and damaging the other ankle!'

Laura's heart began to thud painfully but whether it was caused by fright or some other emotion, she did not have time to determine. In no time at all he had settled her at the table and then he reached forward and lit the candle.

The candle gave a gentle, flickering light and the firelight glowed in the hearth, the flames casting dancing shadows around the room. The howling of the wind outside the cottage only served to make the atmosphere more enchanting.

For a moment neither of them spoke. Eventually Laura glanced up at him. What with the dim light and his abundant beard it was more difficult than ever to read his expression but Laura could have sworn that he looked sad.

Then he saw her looking at him and he grinned.

'I'll go and get the food – it should all be ready.'

'Wait–'

He turned. 'Yes?'

'Why are you doing this?'

'What do you mean?'

'Why have you gone to so much bother to make this meal attractive?'

'You haven't tasted the food yet!'

'Oh, please be serious – you know what I mean!'

'Of course I do, Laura. I'll try to explain. You and I trapped here together in un-pleasant circumstances – I don't know for how long – and I just wanted to lighten the atmosphere a bit – there's no point in us both being thoroughly miserable, is there?'

'I see.'

Laura was silent. She had suddenly thought of her father. He, too, would have felt obliged to make the best of bad circumstances. Once more, she suspected that he would have liked this man – but how could you like a murderer?

Luckily, Julian North did not see the blush that stained her cheek. She need not have worried that he would read her thoughts again for he was half-way to the kitchen. She heard him clatter about with the pots and pans and she made a determined effort to compose herself before he came back.

He brought in a tray with two covered casserole dishes on it. He placed the dishes on the table and sat down. The smell was delicious and Laura wrinkled her nose and smiled in anticipation. Julian reached forward and simultaneously lifted both lids with a flourish.

One dish contained creamy white pasta with a knob of butter still melting in the steam on top, and the other held a rich, red sauce. Julian smiled, pleased at Laura's reaction.

She gasped. 'How did you do it? I mean, I know I brought a packet of dried spaghetti with me, but the sauce – it smells fantastic!'

'It was easy. I rummaged around in the boxes of groceries you brought and I found onions, a green pepper, some mushrooms and a couple of tins of chopped tomatoes.'

'That doesn't account for the wonderful smell!'

'Well, I found some jars of dried herbs in the kitchen cupboard–'

'They were my mother's–' Laura interrupted.

'And as a final touch I'm afraid I used about a third of your bottle of wine. Do you mind?'

'Wine?'

'Yes, in amongst the tinned beans and the packets of biscuits I found a bottle of cheap, red wine. It didn't look fit for anything else so I guessed you intended to use it for cooking. Oh, no – have I made a *faux pas?*'

Laura was blushing. Steve had bought her the wine. Laura had known it was only a cheap wine but she hadn't said anything. She was far too kind and well brought up ever to have hurt his feelings. At the time she had thought he simply didn't know much about wine and, anyway, it wasn't important.

Now she was not so sure. Perhaps Steve had always brought cheap wine because that's how he valued her. In the few months they had known each other he had never taken her out. They had always gone to her apartment on the quayside and cooked a meal together, watched television or listened to music.

Steve had said it was because he needed to be alone with her away from the world. Laura knew now why they never went anywhere – it was because he was a married man.

Julian reached across the table and took her hand.

'I'm a prize fool, aren't I? You don't have to tell me what I've said to make you look so sad – I've already guessed. Your boyfriend bought you the wine, didn't he, and I've just insulted it. Well I take back everything I've said. That bottle of wine has helped to make us a delicious meal and when I was a student I couldn't have afforded anything better either.'

'What makes you say that – about being a student?'

'I'm guessing that that's what you are and that would make your boyfriend a student, too. Am I right?'

'No,' Laura smiled wanly. 'You're not quite right, but don't let's waste any more time talking. Let's eat this delicious meal you've prepared!'

Julian grinned. 'And now that it's open, shall we drink up the wine?'

'No, I've got a much better bottle of wine in the cupboard under the stairs. Several bottles, in fact. My father fitted it out like a little wine cellar – you go and choose something – I'll trust your judgement.'

Julian went along with the Italian theme and chose a bottle of Chianti Classico, one of her mother's favourites, she remembered, and perhaps it was under the influence of the tasty food and full red wine but soon they were chatting like old friends.

They talked about music they liked, books they had read and some of the places they had seen. Laura sensed that Julian North was deliberately keeping the conversation light but she didn't mind. She even began to enjoy herself.

For afters he had managed to find a tin of peaches and some evaporated milk. This was followed by cheese and biscuits. Laura realized they had finished the bottle of wine between them.

When they were sipping their coffee Julian said, 'We'd be more comfortable by the fire.'

He pushed the table back and pulled the

sofa up to the hearth once more, and they settled down with their coffee.

The candle had burnt low and spluttered out in a pool of wax. Now the only illumination was the warm glow of the fire. As Laura sipped her coffee the light shone in her copper-coloured hair. Julian North was silent as he looked at her.

Then, as she leaned forward to put her empty cup on the floor, he said, 'Those are pretty earrings you're wearing Laura. Did you buy them locally?'

'I didn't buy them – I made them. You were almost right about my being a student. I only completed my course in design this summer. I'm working now, designing and manufacturing jewellery.'

'Where? In London?'

'No, in Newcastle. I work for Chris Martin at the Blackfriars Craft Centre.'

Laura faltered. She remembered Maxine's spiteful outburst. Maxine's father was a big wholesaler and one of the workshop's biggest customers. Laura wondered what her boss would do if Maxine carried out her threat to get her father to stop placing orders if he continued to use Laura's designs.

'Does your boyfriend work there too?'

Laura didn't think it was the right time to

tell this man about her precise relationship with Steve Fraser so she simply replied, 'No, Steve is a buyer for one of our customers, a big wholesaler.'

'So you met at the workshop?'

'Yes, he was very taken with my designs – in fact his support really got me started...'

It was true, Laura reflected sadly. She supposed she would never know Steve's reasons for singling out her designs but, whatever had happened since, she wanted to believe it was for the best of motives – because her work was good.

'And will they be wondering where you are?'

'Who?'

'Your colleagues at the craft centre – surely they'll be wondering why you haven't been to work?'

'Oh, no. They're not expecting me back until after the Christmas holiday. You see we've been tremendously busy getting the Christmas orders out – everyone's been working just about all around the clock – and suddenly we realized we'd done it. All the orders were delivered and there was plenty of stock left over for last minute fill-ups. Chris told me to disappear until the new year and dream up some new designs for spring.'

'And will you?'

'Mmm?'

'Will you dream up some new designs?'

'I suppose so.' Laura frowned. She had already started work on her new designs but she was not sure if Chris – or anyone else – would want them now. Not after what Maxine had said.

Julian stared thoughtfully. The girl looked troubled and he guessed that it would be because of Steve and whatever had happened between them. He also guessed that probably no one was missing her – with any luck no one would come looking for her yet.

But it would be unwise to relax. He could not be sure that her boyfriend would not come running after her. And he could not be sure that he had evaded those who were pursuing him. It was time to take action.

SIX

When Laura woke up a steady drip of water from the melting snow on the roof told her that the thaw had begun.

Bright sunshine was streaming through the gap in the curtains. She sat up, pushed down the bedclothes and then stopped and groaned softly.

She remembered that they had drunk a full bottle of red wine between them the night before and she was suffering for it now. She smiled faintly; she reckoned a headache was a small price to pay for the good meal and the interesting conversation. Last night was the first time she had been able to relax for days – for a while she had almost forgotten the predicament she was in. The dark, forbidding man who was taking refuge in her cottage had seemed almost human.

Or had he? Laura frowned as she remembered that the evening had ended in a puzzling way. Everything had been fine until they had taken their coffee to sit by the fire.

They had been chatting like old friends. He had persuaded her to talk about her work and it was when she had been telling him about her time off to design the spring range that the atmosphere had changed.

Laura thought it might have been her fault. She remembered staring into the fire moodily as she contemplated her future and whether anyone would actually want those designs if Maxine carried out her threat.

But Julian North had been silent, too. When she looked up he had been staring at her intently and then, quite suddenly, his expression had changed. It was as if he had made an important decision.

He had not said anything. He had settled the fire and put up the guard and then cleared the table and taken the dirty plates into the kitchen. He had not allowed her to help.

When he returned he had been carrying the hot water bottles.

'Up to bed with you, Laura. You need your rest; if the thaw sets in it's going to be a busy day tomorrow.'

She had not made any objection. Full of good food and wine and warmed by the fire she had been sleepy and ready to obey.

Now, as she opened the curtains and gazed out at the melting snow, she wondered how he had guessed that the weather would change. And what had he meant about it being a busy day? She had better get dressed and go down.

She paused at the top of the stairs. She could hear a woman's voice again and this time she knew she was not dreaming. Although the voice was low, it was articulate and confident. Someone was here in the cottage and it must be a friend of Julian North.

Laura went down the stairs as carefully as she could but she still could not put too much weight on her right ankle so she was clumsy and she made more noise than she intended. By the time she reached the bottom the voice had stopped.

She gazed around the living-room. There was no one there, but the door which led into the kitchen was ajar. She could hear him moving about but before she could take another step, the door opened wide and he came into the room towards her. He was smiling.

'I heard you coming down so I've started cooking breakfast. Did you sleep well?'

'Who's here?'

'I beg your pardon?'

'There's somebody else in the cottage. Who is it?'

'You're mistaken, Laura, we're alone.'

'You're lying – I heard someone talking – in the kitchen–'

Suddenly, Laura lost her patience and pushed past him. She had no sense of fear.

The kitchen was empty. The back door was closed and bolted, last night's dishes were clean and still lying on the draining board, some rashers of bacon were sizzling in the frying pan, but there was nobody there.

And then Laura saw what she should have been looking for in the first place. On the bench, next to the teapot, stood the radio. The voice she had heard for the last two mornings had been that of a newsreader.

He came into the kitchen.

'That's how you knew about the change in the weather – you heard the forecast.' She looked at him accusingly.

'I wasn't trying to hide your radio, Laura. You could have had it if you'd asked for it, but I just needed to keep up to date with the–' he faltered.

'With the news. I know, there's no need to tell me why, I can guess.'

'Go and sit down at the table. We'll have breakfast and then we'll talk.'

Laura enjoyed her breakfast. The simple fare of bacon and beans and toast and tea was all the more enjoyable because it was served in front of the fire in the cosy little cottage room.

As she sipped her tea, she marvelled, once more, that in spite of the impossible situation, she could feel comfortable in this man's company. And she could tell that he was at ease with her. Perhaps it was propinquity, after all. They both had their problems, although his were much greater than hers. Who could blame either of them for enjoying this brief respite?

He had brought the radio through and they had been listening while they had been eating. Now it was time for a news bulletin.

It was still the lead item. There was no new information but the piece ended with an appeal.

'The police are convinced that someone is giving this man refuge,' the newsreader said, 'and they urge anyone who may have information to come forward.'

He reached over and turned off the radio and then he turned to look at her with raised eyebrows.

'Well, any questions?'

'Why didn't you bring your own radio?'

'What?' he laughed. 'I'm not sure what I was expecting, but certainly not that!'

'Maybe not, but it's a good question. I mean, whatever your plans were when you came here, you must have realized that you would have to know what was going on – unless – unless…'

'Don't worry, Laura. I wasn't planning to do away with myself!'

'So, why no radio?'

'I did pack one but I think S – someone must have taken it out of my haversack when we were in the car.'

'The car?'

'We – I left London in my wife's car. Why not? It was sitting in the garage round the corner from our apartment. We don't own the garage, we rent it from a large, anonymous company so the police probably don't even realize, yet, that the car is missing. And when they do discover its loss, they'll never find it.'

Laura's head was reeling. He had admitted so much and yet so little. She knew that there had been someone with him when he got away from London – and that someone was probably a woman. Also this woman had taken his radio – his means of keeping in touch with the outside world – but if she was a friend why would she do that?

He had not said anything about the ghastly events which led up to his flight but he had been able to talk calmly about taking his wife's car. Could he have done so if he had just battered her to death?

Laura blanched. She knew that some men would be able to do that. She glanced up into his face to find him looking at her with concern.

'Well, any more questions?'

Suddenly, Laura knew that the question she had been dreading need not be asked. She did not believe that Julian North could voluntarily kill anyone – let alone his wife.

'Yes, I have one more question. How can I help you?'

Julian reached across the table and took both of her hands in his.

'Bless you, Laura. Bless you for believing in me but you can't help.'

'What are you going to do?'

'I can't tell you that. It's better that you know as little as possible.'

A log stirred and shifted in the fire and he

got up and went over to the hearth. He bent to settle it and make it safe. The firelight glowed on his dark hair and tanned skin. Laura went over to stand beside him.

When he straightened up she put both her hands on his shoulders and looked up into his eyes.

'Julian, last night, I don't know why but I got the impression that you had reached some decision. Just before I went up to bed I thought you might be going to ask me something.'

'You're right, Laura. Perhaps it was the meal we had together, the intimate atmosphere, but I had this crazy idea of asking you for help. However, now, in the cold light of day, I know it would be grossly unfair of me to do so.'

'But you have a plan?'

'Yes – a plan of sorts.'

'And is it dangerous – for me, I mean?'

'Probably.'

'And if you don't carry it out – what would happen then?'

Suddenly Julian pulled her into the circle of his arms. 'Oh, my dear,' he groaned. 'You're right, that could be just as dangerous for you. Time is running out – we must act quickly. Sit down, here by the fire

– we have to talk.'

As the snow melted, the steep mountain road became a small stream and Laura's car swooshed down, sending up sprays of water mixed with small lumps of ice.

Julian was driving. He was wearing her father's parka with the hood up and pulled well forward to conceal his face, whereas Laura had made no attempt to disguise her identity.

The sun was bright and the inside of the car was warm. Laura felt beads of perspiration gathering on her brow but she knew the cause was nervous tension rather than the heat.

Once they reached the bottom of the track they found that the road that led into the village was almost clear of snow, although there were great heaps of it at each side where the snow ploughs had pushed it. They looked like piles of brown sugar sparkling in the sunlight.

There were a few people about in the village street and one or two of them glanced at Laura's car as they slowed down and parked outside the general store.

Incredible as it might seem, the first part of Julian's plan was a shopping expedition.

Julian turned to her and smiled encouragingly. 'Right, you know what to do, off you go.'

She grinned and reached forward to adjust the hood of the parka. 'You'll ruin everything if you let that beard show – or rather, you'll ruin my reputation and I'll never be able to face my friends in the village again!'

As she closed the car door and hobbled into the shop she wondered how she could feel so lighthearted – especially when every step was proving so painful. Perhaps it was a sign of hysteria. She would have to be careful.

She was the only customer. Mrs Charlton was sitting behind the counter with her knitting and she looked up and smiled.

'Laura! We saw the smoke from the chimney so we thought you must be at the cottage. We were quite worried about you – if you hadn't turned up soon, Archie was going to go up and see if you were OK.'

So Julian had been right. He knew that the cottage was visible from the houses that lay on the north side of the village street and he guessed that the people who lived there would have seen that it was occupied.

He had wanted Laura to establish that the occupier was the lawful owner and that she was perfectly safe before anyone came to investigate. That explained the first part of his plan.

But Mrs Charlton was looking concerned. 'Did I see you limping, Laura? Have you had an accident and are you all alone up there?'

'No, no accident, I turned my ankle at work the other day but it's nothing serious. And I'm not alone, I've brought a friend along – a friend from the craft centre. She's waiting in the car, she's got a bit of a cold and she doesn't want to risk making it worse by getting out.'

'Poor little lass. Why didn't she just stay in the cottage?'

'She didn't want me to make the journey alone.'

Laura suddenly had an irrepressible urge to giggle. The idea of Julian North being called a 'poor little lass' was too much for her. She snorted and attempted to turn it into a cough.

'You're not catching a cold, too, are you, dear?'

'I hope not. But, Mrs Charlton, I've got such a long list here, I wonder if you'd help me? You see we plan to stay at the cottage for a few days – maybe even over Christmas

– so we'll need lots of provisions.'

Mrs Charlton took the list Laura gave her and began bustling about the shop collecting the assortment of goods from the shelves.

Laura left her to it and went over to the newspaper and magazine stand. She pretended to look at the magazines for a while and then chose one at random. She had been putting off the moment of choosing the newspapers because she was frightened to look at the headlines. Eventually she just snatched the papers that Julian had asked for, folded them over and took them back to the counter.

Mrs Charlton was just finishing packing Laura's shopping into a large cardboard box. She glanced at Laura thoughtfully and, eventually, she said, 'Haven't you got anywhere else to go for Christmas, dear? You know you and your pal could always come down and spend the day with Archie and me.'

'That's very kind of you but I don't think we can. You see the reason we're here is because we're working on the new spring designs – my jewellery, you know – and we need peace and quiet and no distractions.'

Mrs Charlton stopped work for a moment and smiled sadly at Laura. 'Your parents would have been so proud of you. But what would they have thought of me if I let you spend Christmas all alone in the cottage?'

'But I won't be alone – my friend J-Julia is here, remember?'

Mrs Charlton looked unconvinced so Laura hurried on, 'Look, I'll come down for a quick visit on Christmas Day, I promise–'

'And your friend too.'

'Y-yes, she'll come if she's feeling better. Now, if that's everything, I'll settle up with you and set off for home. I think my friend has probably been out long enough.'

Laura carried the heavy box of groceries out to the car. It was agonizing but she had to walk as normally as possible otherwise she knew Mrs Charlton would insist on helping her. She was grateful that another customer came in and Mrs Charlton was distracted. She knew that, given the chance, the kind woman would come out to the car and try to chat to 'Julia'.

Once she was settled inside the car, Julian reached out and took her hand. 'Sorry I couldn't help you, I forgot how painful your ankle was.'

Laura didn't reply; she simply lay back in her seat and closed her eyes; but they were well away from the village before she felt able to relax. Then she let out a heartfelt sigh.

'What's the matter?' Julian glanced at her briefly and then turned his attention back to the road.

'You were right about them guessing I was at the cottage but we should have realized that Mrs Charlton would want to help. We couldn't have known that another customer would turn up at just the right moment. What on earth would you have done if she'd come out to the car?'

'I should have buried my nose in a bundle of tissues and sneezed non-stop!'

Laura began to giggle.

'Why are you laughing?'

'I hope you can sneeze in a ladylike fashion – Julia!'

'So that's my name, now is it?' He began to laugh and soon both of them were helpless. It wasn't until he turned the car up into the fellside track that they sobered down sufficiently to carry on with their conversation.

'Seriously, Julian, she expects us to visit her on Christmas Day. She knew my parents and I suppose she feels sorry for me.'

Julian peered ahead. The short winter day

meant that the sky was darkening again.

'Do you mind?'

'I don't know what you mean.'

'Poor kid, you've had a rough time. Do you mind when people feel sorry for you?'

'I've never thought about it – I mean, I've kept my own company since my parents died – I suppose I've been a bit isolated, until I met Steve, that is...'

'Oh, yes, Steve.'

Did Laura imagine it or did Julian grip the steering wheel more tightly? He didn't speak again until they pulled up outside the cottage.

He turned and looked at her. 'I'm going inside first and I want you to wait here – it's important.'

He was gone leaving Laura feeling puzzled. Why had he gone in without her and why hadn't he explained? Suddenly she thought she knew and she was very angry. She was shaking when he returned and opened her door.

'Searching the cottage were you?' she almost shouted.

'Yes, how did you guess?'

'Did you think I'd betrayed you? Did you think I'd told Mrs Charlton all about you the minute I got inside the shop? Were you worried the police would be waiting for you?'

'Laura, stop this!'

He pulled her up into his arms roughly and then he gentled her as if she were a child until she calmed down a little.

'You're not talking sense, Laura. If you'd told Mrs Charlton who I was you wouldn't have come out of that shop again. The police would have arrived in their Range Rover and I would have been off like a shot in this car.

'I'm not denying that it crossed my mind that that might happen but the odds were that it wouldn't.'

'Why do you say that?'

He took hold of her face with both of his hands and tilted it up so that she was looking into his eyes.

'Because I trust you.'

They looked at each other for a long time and then Laura shivered.

'Cold, sweetheart?'

Her heart leapt to hear him call her that but she went on. 'No, I'm worried. If it wasn't the police you were expecting, why were you searching the cottage?'

'I can't tell you. Please, don't ask.'

If Laura had been nervous before, now she

was terrified and it was because of the emotion she had just glimpsed in his eyes – Julian North was afraid.

SEVEN

Laura was subdued as they unpacked the shopping in the kitchen. Julian moved about the small room quietly and efficiently and as he did so he kept up a flow of cheerful chatter. Had she been imagining the fear in his eyes?

Soon the food was stacked neatly in the pantry, with the cartons of milk, butter, cheeses and yoghurts and the like going into the small and ancient fridge which Laura's father had managed to fit in by taking out the two bottom shelves.

'Whose idea was this?' Julian sounded amused and Laura turned round in surprise.

He had just finished emptying one of the boxes and he was folding up some cellophane packets of Christmas streamers and decorations.

'I didn't put these on the list,' he continued. 'Did you?'

'No,' Laura went to join him. 'I wonder if Mrs Charlton put them in by mistake?'

'Wait, here's something else in the bottom

111

of the box – a card, I think. It's addressed to you.'

He handed it over and Laura opened it, a bemused smile on her face.

It was a cheerful, traditional Christmas card, showing a picture of a stage coach loaded with jolly passengers and brightly wrapped parcels, the horses galloping bravely through the snowbound countryside of long ago.

Inside, Mrs Charlton had written, 'To Laura and her friend, Julia, love from Archie and Anne Charlton'.

Written on the back of the card, Laura found a further message: 'The decorations are a little gift. Remember, you're both welcome at our house on Christmas Day!'

Laura looked worried. 'If I don't go down there for my Christmas dinner, I think Archie might very well come up and get me. Then what will you do?'

'I could always retire upstairs to bed and you could say your friend "Julia's" cold had got worse and you didn't want to leave her.'

'Mr Charlton would go right back to the village and send the doctor up.'

'Don't look so worried, Laura.' Julian pulled her into his arms and attempted to smooth the wrinkles that were forming on her brow. 'It's my problem, not yours, and I've got over a week to plan something. Anyway, we may not be here by then.'

'Not here? But what about all this food you've bought? There's bacon, eggs, tinned food, biscuits – why, you even put a small Christmas cake and a box of mince pies on the list. You must have intended us to be here on the 25th!'

He looked grave. 'Laura, I just can't tell you where I might be by then, but, remember you and your fictional friend, Julia, are supposed to be staying here over Christmas so you had to buy plenty of food and, also, if the weather worsens again I might have no choice but to stay with you.

'Now, I've put the kettle on. Do you think you could manage to make a pot of tea and make us some sandwiches with this delicious Cumberland roast ham? I'll fetch some more logs in and see to the fire.'

As Laura made the tea and sandwiches she could not help noticing how Julian scanned the fellside through the kitchen window before going out for the logs. Who did he think was out there?

She cut up a small Dundee cake and put it on the tray with the sandwiches and tea things. When everything was ready she picked up the tray. It was heavy and her ankle was still painful. She hobbled through into the sitting-room.

It had been transformed. The fire was blazing cheerily and pinpoints of light were reflecting from the tinsel streamers that Julian had hung about the room.

He had placed the Christmas card in the centre of the mantelpiece and arranged a couple of sprays of plastic holly at each side of it. He turned and grinned. 'I'd rather have real evergreens to deck our hall with but seeing Mrs Charlton has been so kind as to send these, I might as well use them. Here, let me take that tray before you drop it!'

Julian placed the tray carefully on the table and, taking hold of Laura's hands, he pulled her gently into his arms.

'Why have you done all this?' she murmured.

'I'm not sure. I think it's because everything is so uncertain. I don't know what's going to happen to me, Laura, but I do know that if I had a choice, I would've liked to spend Christmas with you. So just in case anything goes wrong – no, don't say anything – just in case we can't be together at Christmas, I want us to enjoy what time we have as much as we can.

'Look,' he pointed up towards the light hanging in the centre of the room. A sprig of plastic mistletoe was pinned to the lampshade. 'That was in the packet with the holly – plastic, or not, I don't think we should waste it.'

And then his lips came down on hers. He was gentle at first but as he sensed her response his kiss became more demanding. His arms tightened around her waist and Laura's own arms reached up and pulled him as close to her as possible.

She could hear the fire crackling but she lost all sense of space and time as the kiss went on and on. She hardly knew the moment when they sank on to the sofa behind them, his body covering hers. She could feel his arousal.

But then, abruptly, he tore himself away from her. She heard him groan.

For a moment they were both silent and then, he said, softly, 'Laura, my darling, please forgive me.'

'There's nothing to forgive. I wanted you to kiss me.'

'But I have no right to kiss you. No right to hold you – no right to forget the situation I'm in.'

'But, Julian–'

'No, Laura,' his voice was firm. 'There's no point in even discussing it.'

He stood up and went over to the table to pour the tea.

When they had finished eating they cleared up together and took the tray back into the kitchen to wash the dishes.

'Would you mind if I had a glass of whisky, Laura? I noticed you have a bottle in the cupboard under the stairs.'

'Of course – go ahead.'

Laura was surprised. She was not surprised that a man should drink whisky but the request had been so sudden and his manner of asking had been so serious. They had both been quiet as they ate their meal: both aware of what had happened and what could have happened. In view of this, Laura wondered if Julian needed the whisky to revive his flagging spirits.

When she sat down again near the fire, she found that he had placed the bottle of whisky on a small tray with two glasses.

'I thought you might like one, too. To keep me company.'

She sensed the tension in his voice and was suddenly afraid.

'What is it, Julian? Please tell me what's wrong!'

'Nothing – at least nothing that wasn't wrong before. It's just that I think it's time I examined the papers and I need some false courage!'

He picked up the bundle of newspapers from the chair where they had placed them when they first came in. Laura had wondered why he had put this item on the shopping list. They had been listening to every news bulletin on the radio to keep up to date with his situation so Laura could not imagine why he had needed the papers as well.

He began to sort through them. She watched with a puzzled frown as he tore out some of the pages and arranged them on the table. He scrutinized them closely, but he did not explain what he was doing.

Laura sipped her whisky and welcomed the fiery warmth. In spite of the blazing fire she felt cold with apprehension. Eventually, she could stand the silence no longer and she went over to stand behind him. She held on to the back of his chair for support and looked over his shoulder.

He had arranged the torn pieces of paper in some sort of order and Laura saw immediately that it was not the text that he was studying. It was the photographs. There

117

were coloured photographs from the tab-loids and black and white from the quality press, but the scenes they showed were not much different.

Some showed the police guard mounted outside the apartment house in Belgravia and some were pictures of Julian, his wife, Geraldine and their daughter, Sally.

Laura had to grip the chair more tightly as she tried to control the trembling that had overtaken her.

The picture of Julian showed the face she remembered from seeing him on television programmes. Dark, strong features, intelligent eyes and, of course, he was without the beard.

'Have you seen this man?' was the caption under one of the pictures. No one must know that Julian North had since grown a beard, or surely the newspapers would have asked an artist to draw a beard on to one of the photographs.

Geraldine North was breathtakingly beautiful: small and blonde and extremely glamorous. She laughed up at Julian in a shot of them leaving some society ball and she stared confidently at the camera in a more formal pose.

There was a picture of the three of them

together, Julian, Geraldine and Sally. It must have been taken on a holiday by the sea. They sat on the beach with their picnic and beach toys like any normal family. It was a happy snapshot and yet Laura found it the most shocking thing she had seen so far because, for the first time since she had met him, it made her think beyond the obvious.

She realized, then, that although she had come to believe that Julian could not have killed his wife, she had never questioned the fact that he had shown no sorrow. A man who had lost his much-loved wife ought to be grieving, oughtn't he?

But then, who was to say he was not, just because there were no outward signs of grief? When she had lost her parents she had made a point of not breaking down, of not letting her friends guess at the anguish she was trying to hide.

How grateful she had been to Steve for his kindness and his breezy way of doing things. She had come to rely on him coming back and spending time with her in her apartment. Perhaps that's why she had imagined herself in love with him. She knew, now, that it had not been the real thing: any more than Julian North's attraction to her was the real thing.

She guessed that it was simply because he needed some warmth and human affection, just as she had needed Steve.

There was a sudden spluttering in the fire, and a log shifted and fell, sending ash scattering out across the hearth. Julian went quickly to deal with the small crisis, and by the time he returned, Laura had pulled up another chair and was sitting by the table.

He didn't question her action. He simply went on looking at the photographs. Laura watched him. It was not the family shots that interested him, he was examining the pictures of the outside of his house and the longer shots of the fashionable, London square.

'I don't suppose you've got a magnifying glass, here in this cottage?'

The question took Laura by surprise.

'As a matter of fact, I have. But why do you want it?'

'The quality of these prints isn't too good – some magnification might help.'

Laura sighed in exasperation. He had answered her question and yet he hadn't answered it. She already knew he wanted to look at the photographs more closely but the question she had wanted him to answer was, 'Why?'

'The magnifying glass is upstairs, in the cupboard in my bedroom. I used to collect stamps when I was younger and my things are still here. I don't know how good it will be – it's a toy, really.'

'Don't you attempt the stairs, Laura. I'll go.'

While he was gone, Laura reached forward and took one of the photographs. Her eye had been caught by the happy features of the child. Sally was going to be as beautiful as her mother and she had inherited her blonde hair. It hung, long and straight, like a fall of silk. She looked like a picture of Alice in Wonderland.

Laura frowned. Where was Sally now? The papers were still full of concern for the missing child. She heard him coming downstairs and she pushed the photograph back across the table; she did not want to seem to be prying.

Whatever it was Julian North was looking for, he did not appear to find it. After examining each one with the magnifying glass, he pushed it aside and shook his head almost imperceptibly.

Then, suddenly, he stood up, gathered them all together and strode across the room to throw them into the fire.

121

He stood with one arm on the mantelpiece and watched gloomily as the fire consumed them.

'Julian, who were you looking for in those photographs?'

He turned to face her and his voice was sharp. 'What made you think I was looking for someone?'

'I can't think of any other reason why you should examine the area where you live so closely. It seemed to me that when you had the magnifying glass you were examining the faces in the crowd – the reporters, the onlookers, even the policemen.'

'Very astute.'

'Well, who is it? Is it the same person that you thought might be in the cottage when we returned today? Or, for that matter, is it the same person you thought I might be when I arrived and you nearly throttled the life out of me? Whoever it is, Julian, I know that you're afraid of him.'

He crossed the room swiftly and sat down at the table. Reaching out, he took both of Laura's hands in his and he stared into her eyes.

'Yes, I'm afraid, Laura. Even more now that you are unwittingly involved. I can't tell you anything – it's safer for you if you remain ignorant. I've failed once, God help me, I mustn't fail again.'

Laura stared at him in consternation. She had never been so frightened in her life and yet she realized that she trusted this man – would trust him with her life. She knew, now, that the stakes were that high.

'Julian – there's something that I have to know–' she broke off when she found him gripping her hands more tightly.

'What is it?'

'Your daughter – Sally – is she safe?'

Julian sighed. 'I think so. The police haven't found her. In fact, from the news reports, it's obvious that they haven't got the first idea where she is. So, if the police and the press don't know where Sally is, there's a good chance that–'

'No one else knows, either,' Laura finished the sentence for him.

'That's right.'

He didn't expand and Laura didn't expect him to. She was taken completely aback by his next question.

'Would you like to meet her?'

'Who? Sally?'

'Yes, my daughter, Sally. I'm sure you two will get along famously.'

'Of course I'd like to meet her but how

could that be possible? Oh, I see, you don't mean right now, do you? You mean some time in the future when all this is over.'

Julian was grinning. 'I'm glad to see that you've still got faith in me – that it's all going to be over some day, but, no, I don't mean some time in the distant future. I mean in the very near future. Tonight for example!'

'Tonight?'

Julian suddenly became serious. 'Remember, I said I had a plan? A lot depends on circumstance, but after we've listened to the next news bulletin on the radio, I may decide it's time to move on. If I do, I've got to see Sally first and I don't want to leave you alone in the cottage.'

'But after you've seen Sally – what then?'

'We'll both be coming back here for a while.'

'And then?'

'I can't tell you.'

Laura knew it was useless to question him further. He had a habit of giving out as much information as he wished and then cutting off. She would have to trust him.

'All right, I'll come with you.'

Their little world became even smaller for the next few hours as they tended the fire, made various hot drinks for themselves and listened to the news on the radio.

Laura did not know exactly what he was listening out for but she tried very hard to work out whether the situation had changed with each subsequent report. She did not think it had.

As the day drew to its close, Julian insisted that they cook a proper meal for themselves and they tried valiantly to chat about other things.

Sitting at the table over coffee, after the meal, Julian said, 'Do you think you could tell me about Steve, now?'

Laura flushed. 'Why – why do you want to know?'

Julian took her hand. 'It must be obvious to you that I – that I'm fond of you – even if I have no right to be. Anything that makes you unhappy concerns me.'

Suddenly, Laura found it was easy to talk. She told him anything he didn't already know about her parents' death, her time at college, her loneliness. How Steve had come into her life and brightened it up enormously until that awful moment, just a few nights ago, when Maxine had stormed into her apartment.

She told him everything Maxine had said

and how ashamed that had made her feel: even though she knew now that the shame was entirely Steve's.

She had set out for her cottage to get over what she thought of as a heartbreak, but she had discovered that her heart was not broken after all. Not yet. She didn't tell him that it very well could be – but for an entirely different reason.

When he spoke he said something so unexpected that she simply sat and stared at him.

'Poor Maxine.'

Laura was surprised. 'What did you say?'

'I said, poor Maxine. Imagine what it must be like to be married to someone you can't trust? From what you've told me, you weren't the first girl that Steve betrayed her with – no, listen, Laura.

'I know that you were completely innocent, probably all Steve's victims were. There's obviously something very wrong with their marriage and he's chosen the worst way possible to solve his problems. Just think of the humiliation Maxine must have suffered, time and time again. Don't you see why I feel sorry for her?'

'Y-yes, I suppose I do. But what about my job?'

'I don't think you should let that pair of spoilt children force you to quit.'

'But if she carries out her threat and gets her father to stop placing orders, it will hurt all my friends at the craft centre!'

'I don't think she'd do that. She'd have to admit the truth to her father and my guess is he'd sack that husband of hers. I think that's the last thing she wants – otherwise why is she going to so much bother to hang on to him?'

Laura did not know whether she was convinced but she found she felt much more optimistic. She was to remember some time later how passionately he had spoken about the feelings of humiliation that were inflicted by an unfaithful partner.

EIGHT

It seemed to Laura that there were no new facts emerging from the news bulletins. Geraldine North had been murdered in her luxury home in Belgravia, her daughter, Sally, was missing and her husband and Sally's father, Julian North, the well-known television reporter, could not be contacted although it was known he had returned to England on the night of the killing.

This was the third evening that Laura had been alone with him in the cottage. She sipped her cocoa and stared pensively into the flames. Was it only four days ago that Maxine had swept into her apartment and completely overturned her life?

She had spent that night driving through the desolate countryside towards what she thought was going to be her personal sanctuary. She had not known that dawn would bring her an altogether different set of problems.

She became aware that Julian had turned up the volume on the radio set. It was nearly time for the nine o'clock news.

Still partly lost in her own thoughts she was only half listening to the catalogue of disasters that seemed to afflict the world at Christmas time. An air crash, a fire in a department store, a child snatched and taken abroad by its own estranged father and, then, the same sad details on the Belgravia murder enquiry. Julian switched the set off.

Laura lay back amongst the cushions and closed her eyes only to open them quickly when he took hold of her shoulders and said, 'Don't go to sleep, Laura. We're going now.'

She stared up into his face in disbelief. 'Going? But I don't understand. What could you have heard to make you decide to go now? As far as I can make out, nothing's changed.'

'Oh, but it has. Didn't you notice my story's not making the headlines anymore? The Belgravia murder has slipped down to fourth item in the news, behind the air disaster, the fire and the child snatch. That means that no new facts have emerged and I'll have to put the next part of my plan into action.'

He turned away from her and began

settling down the fire. When he was sure it was safe, he put the guard up and moved swiftly about the room collecting his belongings and stowing them in his rucksack. It was obvious that he wanted to leave no sign of his presence in the cottage.

When it was all done to his satisfaction he smiled briefly. 'Get yourself wrapped up warmly, Laura. It's a cold night.'

'Do I have to bring my things, too?'

'No, I'm only clearing mine out in case anyone should pay a visit while we're away. Any of your friends from the village, for example. Come along – we'll be back before dawn.'

Laura did not ask him who else he expected might call. She knew he would not tell her.

Julian had not told Laura where they were going but she realized it could not be far away if they were going to be back at the cottage by morning.

So Sally, who was last heard of in her own home just before her mother died, was now in the north country. Laura was guessing that when Julian made his escape from London he had brought his daughter with him. But where had he taken her and where had he left his wife's car before he had walked over the fells to the cottage? Laura would soon know.

They were driving without lights. They had gone down the track almost as far as the village road and then turned off on to the old road that snaked back up into the fells, past the outlying farms, almost as far as the fell top and then wound back down again until it joined the Carlisle road well past the village.

The sky was cloudless and the bright moonlight, reflecting off the snow-covered fells, gave them enough light to drive by.

The car was simply a dark shape moving along between the drystone walls, whereas if they had had their lights on they would have been seen moving across the deserted countryside from miles away.

'When we get back to the main road I'll have to put the lights on. We'll stop at the service station and you can fill the car up while I make a phone-call.'

Julian smiled at her fleetingly. He seemed to know the lay of the land pretty well. But then hadn't he said that he had walked these fells since he had been a boy? Even though she was a good driver, Laura had been happy to let Julian take the wheel and negotiate the mountain roads. And besides –

132

she had no idea where they were going!

She watched him settle himself in the call-box and begin to feed coins into the phone. He had not told her whom he was calling.

'Laura, it's good to see you again! Mrs Charlton told me you were at the cottage.'

She glanced up in dismay at the cheerful young man who was taking her money. The mini-market at the service station was closed and locked but the glass pay-booth, which was part of it, was brightly lit and cheerful with Christmas decorations. The youth who stood there was Ralph Latham, a local boy she had known since her parents first bought the cottage.

'Oh, hi, Ralph. Er – I didn't know you worked here.' Laura couldn't think of what else to say but luckily he didn't notice how ill at ease she was.

'I only work here in the holidays. I'm at university – Lancaster – but I do the night shifts here whenever I'm at home. I need the money!'

'Well,' Laura took her change. 'Nice to see you, but I must be going. It's late.'

'Is that your friend in the phone-box?' Ralph was peering out across the apron of the service station. 'Mrs Charlton said you had a friend with you.'

Laura prayed that Julian would keep his back to them. The hood of the parka was pulled well up but if Ralph glimpsed any part of Julian's beard he would know that Laura wasn't sharing her cottage with a girl friend!

'Yes, that's Julia.' Laura was surprised how convincing she sounded. 'She's phoning her friends in Carlisle. We were supposed to be there earlier but we got delayed – I'm working on my new jewellery designs, you know. So we're just letting them know we're on our way in case they were worrying about us.'

Laura was proud of the story she had concocted on the spur of the moment. As soon as they pulled away from the service station Ralph would notice that they were not heading back towards the cottage.

Ralph was unhappy. 'The roads are pretty bad, if I were you, I would ask your friends if you could stay the night and come back in the morning.'

'Good idea, we'll probably do that.'

Out of the corner of her eye she saw the door of the phone booth opening. She called a cheery goodbye and hurried across to take Julian's arm.

'Keep your head down. I'll tell you all

about it when we're safe inside the car!'

After she had told him about Ralph, he said, 'Bless you, Laura. It's true, I didn't want to leave you alone at the cottage but, by coming with me, you're also providing a cover story. If I didn't have the use of your car I would have had to walk there and back and that might have been dangerous.'

He still didn't say where they were going or who he had been phoning but he did say, 'Nearly there.'

They had not travelled much further when he slowed down and left the main road once more. Then, about two miles along the track he turned the car in between massive, stone pillars. The gateway led to a private drive which wound through a plantation of fir trees.

The house was so far set back from the road that Laura did not wonder that she had not known of its existence.

The old house looked graceful set amongst the bowl of the surrounding hills and the snow-covered lawns. The drive curved around to the grand entrance porch but Julian took the fork which led to the back of the house, where there were several outbuildings. Laura knew without being told that in one of these outbuildings would be found Geraldine North's car.

He parked the car in the shadows and got out.

'Come with me. We're expected.'

The snow had been swept clear from the cobbled courtyard but the stones were slippery. Laura had hardly been bothered by her ankle for the last few hours but now it gave a twinge of pain as she slipped on the treacherous surface.

She could not stop herself from crying out and Julian grasped her hand and pulled her close to him. He kept his arm around her as they headed towards the back door.

He still had not told her exactly whom they would meet inside – Sally could not be staying here on her own. Laura smiled to herself as she wondered if Julian was always the strong, silent type or whether it was his present situation that had made him so economical with explanations.

They didn't have to knock. Someone must have been waiting and watching their progress across the yard because the door swung open as soon as they reached it.

The room was in darkness. Laura glimpsed a shadowy figure beckoning them inside, then Julian shut the door behind them and the light came on.

136

'Julian – I've been so worried about you!'

Laura looked at the woman, who still had her hand on the light switch. She was tall and slim and extremely elegant. Her light brown hair was swept back into a French pleat and she was wearing a figure-hugging red woollen dress. She wore pearls at her neck and in her ears and there was a lingering aroma of expensive perfume.

Julian had moved forward and taken her in his arms. 'Amanda, my love, I'm sorry to cause you so much trouble. You've been absolutely wonderful.'

He hugged her and she lowered her head until it rested on his chest. She closed her eyes but not before Laura had seen the tears in them.

Laura felt weak. She eased herself back until she was resting against the door. They had completely forgotten about her. She did not know how long she stood there but she hardly dared admit to herself what thoughts had leapt into her mind.

There was no denying the emotions that these two were showing. Were those emotions strong enough to kill for?

Reluctantly, it seemed to Laura, they pulled themselves apart and the woman smiled up at him and said, shakily, 'It's been no trouble at all and I'd do anything to help – you must know that.'

Then she drew herself up straight and stepped away from him, and acknowledged Laura's presence for the first time. 'Laura, isn't it?' She was smiling. 'Julian told me about you when he phoned just now. You must have had a dreadful shock when you found him at the cottage!'

Julian looked grave. 'It was very bad luck for Laura to have been drawn into my problems like this. That's one of the reasons I've decided that I must move on. At the moment Laura is an accessory – once I've gone she can tell the police I kept her there against her will – forced her to help me–'

Laura flushed. 'I wouldn't do that because it's not true – I'm helping you because I want to!'

Julian took hold of both her shoulders in his powerful hands. 'That's what you believe, now, Laura. But have you ever heard of kidnap victims being brainwashed? Growing to like or even love their captors? It wouldn't be the first time it had happened to an impressionable girl.'

Laura flushed at his words and stared up into his eyes. She was trying to remember the moment when she had decided that this man was not the enemy she had first supposed him to be. They had been alone together in the cottage, cocooned from the outside world by the weather. What had he said about propinquity...?

Amanda broke the uneasy silence by sighing gently and taking hold of Julian's arm. 'I'm sure Laura is sensible enough to work out for herself what will be the best course of action.'

She smiled kindly. 'I'm Amanda Heron. Julian and I have been friends since we were youngsters growing up in Carlisle.'

Julian was grinning. 'This is the nurse I was telling you about the other day. I'd known her since schooldays – she was just a pal, but I can't tell you what she did to my heart the day I first saw her in her nurse's uniform! She was the sweetest, sexiest sight I'd ever seen.

'Unfortunately Amanda took one look at a certain handsome young medical student and my hopes were dashed forever!'

Laura was bemused – she was trying to imagine this elegant woman dressed in anything except the most expensive clothes – and she certainly didn't smell of disinfectant or antiseptic now!

Julian went on. 'She actually married him!

Douglas Heron – or Sir Douglas as he is now – not only carried off the girl I loved but he went on to become a very distinguished consultant.'

He turned to smile at his former girlfriend. 'Don't you ever regret the life you could have had, married to a roving reporter, Amanda?'

'No – I wouldn't be able to stand the excitement. Your lifestyle is far too dangerous for me; why, Geraldine used to say – oh dear – I shouldn't–' Amanda broke off in confusion.

Julian said brusquely, 'Forget it, Amanda – don't say any more.'

With an effort, she controlled herself. 'We can't stay here in the kitchen – take your outdoor things off and let's go through to the sitting-room. There's a good fire and someone waiting there to see you.'

The house had been well cared for. There were none of the usual draughts or lingering smells of dampness usually found in old buildings. Laura followed the other two along a well-carpeted, softly lit passage into a large, well-proportioned hallway.

Then, just before Amanda opened one of the oak doors, she paused and said quietly, 'I kept Sally up when I knew you were coming. She'll be so pleased to see you.'

Laura wondered how the Herons had explained Sally's presence to their staff and friends.

'One moment before we go in, Julian,' Amanda looked worried. 'I hope you don't mind but I've cut her hair. It was a sin to do it – such beautiful hair – but it was so distinctive – and Sally loves her new style.'

'I'm sure you did what was best, Amanda. Amanda – wait – has she remembered anything?'

'No, I'm sorry, Julian. Douglas and I have been as gentle as possible. We've questioned her tactfully like you said we should, but Sally doesn't remember anything about – anything about that night until the moment you found her hiding in the toy cupboard in her bedroom.'

The child was tucked up in a blanket in a large, comfortable armchair near the fire. The lights from the nearby Christmas tree cast warm reflections across her sleeping face.

She had fallen asleep clutching a small transistor radio. It was still turned on, although the volume was low, and it was tuned in to a programme of light music.

'I'm sorry about the radio, Julian. It must

141

have been difficult for you without one. I didn't realize that Sally had taken it from the car. She thought you had brought it for her – she's been keeping it on her bedside table.'

'Don't worry, Laura had a radio at the cottage. I've been able to follow events.'

Julian was standing over the chair looking down at his daughter. The child stirred in her sleep, then she opened her eyes and looked up. Laura was glad that Julian's back was turned and she could not see his expression. She knew he would want to keep his present feelings private.

Amanda Heron whispered softly, 'Shall we leave them alone for a moment – give father and daughter a chance to get re-acquainted?'

'Of course.'

'Let's go back to the kitchen and make some hot drinks.'

Although Laura had guessed the Herons' had plenty of money, the kitchen was neither smart nor very modern. But it was warm, spotlessly clean and practical. In spite of her appearance, Lady Heron was obviously a competent housewife.

There was an Aga set into a tiled recess where a kettle was gently coming to the boil.

Her hostess put a large tray on the scrubbed pine table and began to set it up. She was very neat. Laura wondered if it was her nursing training.

'It's been wonderful for us to have Sally here. Douglas and I don't have any children, you know.' For a moment Laura thought she glimpsed an expression of pain in the clear, grey eyes.

'But in the present circumstances that's proved a blessing in disguise,' she continued. 'You see, I've become involved with several children's charities over the years and I've often had various youngsters to stay here. We've been able to pass Sally off as one of my "cases".'

'How does Sally feel about that?'

'At the moment it's a game to her,' Amanda frowned. 'We've been calling her Sara, which is her proper name, incidentally, and she's responded to a difficult situation very well. But I hope it won't have to go on much longer. I hope this dreadful business will soon be resolved.'

She had been heating up milk in a small pan, and now she made a mug of hot chocolate. 'I'll just take this through for her. Would you mind making the tea when the kettle boils?'

'Of course not.'

So Sally knew something. It was obvious from his question that Julian suspected that his daughter had been witness to the dreadful events that took place in her home that night – the night her mother was murdered. Poor child – had she seen her mother beaten to death? And, even more terrifying, did she know who had done it? The memory must have been so terrible that she had blanked it out.

There could be a very good reason why Julian North had removed his daughter from London and hidden her away with loyal, old friends in the north country. When, eventually, the child remembered everything that had happened before she took refuge in her toy cupboard, whom exactly would she incriminate?

NINE

'Sally, this is Laura, she's a friend of mine.'

Julian was carrying his daughter in his arms and he had paused at the foot of the stairs when he noticed Laura coming through from the kitchen with the tray.

It was plain from the trusting way Sally snuggled into her father's arms that she did not see him as a threat. Was that because Julian was truly innocent or because Sally could not remember anything that had happened before she left London? Laura frowned. Had she started doubting him again? Did she feel differently because they were away from the enclosed atmosphere of her cottage? Had she really been brainwashed as Julian had suggested?

Sally smiled sleepily; she was still clutching her radio. Laura wondered if it represented something safe from home; something from the days before Sally's world had been turned upside-down.

'I'll take that tray, you look a little shaky,' Amanda had appeared at Laura's elbow.

'No – it's all right, I'm tired, that's all. Just tell me where to put it.'

'Well, if you're sure you're all right, put it in there,' Amanda pointed back into the sitting-room. 'I've pulled a coffee table over near the fire. I'll just go up with Julian and help him settle Sally and then we'll all have a cup of tea together.'

'Good-night, Laura.' Sally surprised them all by calling back down the stairs.

'Good-night, Sally.'

Laura watched them: Julian, carrying his daughter in his arms, and Amanda just behind them talking softly to the child as they went upstairs. She was carrying the mug of hot chocolate. Laura wondered if Amanda had ever regretted turning down her childhood friend. She also wondered where Douglas Heron was tonight and if the scene Laura was witnessing would upset him as much as it was upsetting her.

She forced herself to turn away from them and carry the tray into the sitting-room. She had no right to be jealous.

She was grateful to put the tray down and sit by herself for a moment. It was true that she was tired and, what was more, her ankle was hurting.

Laura tried to put everything out of her

mind and relax. The room was comfortable and the lights were low. The only sounds were the crackling of the flames and occasionally the slight tinkling of the little golden bells on the Christmas tree disturbed by the warm currents of air from the fireplace.

Laura looked at the tree. She wondered if the Herons would have bothered with one if they had not had Sally staying here. Her own parents had always insisted on having all the traditional Christmas decorations no matter to what part of the world they were posted. Laura had had to go to boarding-school but she had always joined her mother and father for holidays. This was the first time she would have to spend Christmas without them.

Her head was aching and the pain in her ankle was getting worse. Julian and Amanda seemed to be taking a long time to put Sally to bed. The tea would be cold and serve them right, Laura thought crossly.

She knew she would have to take a pain-killer. As she made her way to the kitchen the house was so quiet that she fancied it was empty save for herself. What if Julian and Amanda had taken Sally and run away? What would Laura say to Douglas Heron when he came home – if he ever came home? In fact Laura was beginning to wonder if he even existed.

She passed her hand across her brow and realized she was very warm. She must be running a temperature.

The kitchen cupboards were well-stocked and well-organized. Laura soon found a first-aid box, as she had guessed she might, and in it there was a bottle of aspirins.

She took a couple with a long drink of cold water. It was so refreshing that she drank another glassful and then filled it up again to take back with her to the sitting-room. She put the kitchen light out.

She stopped in the doorway. She could hear them talking softly as they came down the stairs. They had no idea that she was there in the shadows.

'You've got to stop blaming yourself, Julian.'

'Amanda, you weren't there – it was like a nightmare!'

'But it wasn't your fault.'

'Of course it was! You're a loyal friend, Amanda, but your feelings for me are blinding you to the truth of the matter – I'm guilty – guilty as hell!'

The icy-cold glass of water began to slip

through Laura's fingers. It was like a film played in slow motion – she knew it was happening and was powerless to stop it. Just as the glass fell and spilled its contents over the Turkey carpet, Laura's knees buckled and she went crashing to the floor.

'I think she's coming round, Julian.'

Laura heard the whispering voices as she turned her face away from the heat of the fire. Julian had carried her through to the sitting-room and placed her in the armchair near the fire; the chair where Sally had been sitting when they first arrived.

'What made her pass out?' That was Julian.

'Well, she does seem to be running a slight fever but I think it was shock – she must have heard what we were saying.'

Amanda had taken Laura's pulse, professionally, like the nurse she had once been. Laura knew this because the efficient Amanda was wrong about one small detail. Laura was not 'coming round' because she had never been 'out'.

She had not fainted as they supposed. When she had felt the glass slipping through her fingers she had not been able to stop an automatic reflex action. She had tried to save it and in doing so stumbled, placing too much weight on her right ankle and then fallen, helplessly.

She had lain there, winded and in pain, and the other two had hurried over and, seeing her closed eyes, assumed that she had fainted. Julian had swung her up into his arms and she had kept her eyes closed, paralyzed with fright – not wanting to look up into his face for fear of what she might see there.

But she'd heard every word they had said.

'Poor Laura. I wonder how long she'd been standing there – how much did she hear?' Was this the voice of a murderer?

'I think you'd better assume the worst, Julian.'

'You know I told her as little as possible, but there was a moment, back there, in the cottage, when I sensed that she believed in my innocence. There and then she offered to help me – I haven't had to coerce her.'

Laura moved restlessly. She could no longer keep up the pretence; she opened her eyes. Julian was frowning and staring into the fire but Amanda met Laura's troubled gaze. She turned and placed a warning hand on Julian's shoulder. 'She's awake and listening to us, Julian. I think the time has come to tell her the truth.'

That had been hours ago.

'We'd better go now, Amanda.' Julian stretched his long legs out towards the dying fire and yawned.

'Don't you think you should get some sleep before you drive back?'

'I could drive – after all, it is my car.'

Amanda smiled at Laura. 'But you haven't had any sleep, either! No, I think you should both rest before you return to the cottage.'

They had talked all night and it would soon be dawn.

'No, it would be awkward for you if your staff arrived before we got safely away. It's better that we get back to the cottage before it's light, then we can both sleep as long as we want to.'

'I suppose you're right, but is there anything I can give you to make life there a little easier?'

'We've got everything we need. Just look after Sally for me.'

'I will, don't worry about her and as soon as Douglas gets back from Edinburgh, I'll let you know as planned.'

Laura frowned. Her head was aching and her mind was spinning with everything she had been told. She watched as Julian sat

151

forward and dropped his head into his hands. It was a weary gesture.

She believed his story implicitly. He had not killed his wife – and yet nothing could persuade him that he was not responsible for her death. In his own eyes he was guilty.

He stood up. 'I'll go up and kiss Sally goodbye – I won't wake her, but I must just see her. I don't know when we'll be together again – certainly not for Christmas.'

'Douglas and I will make Christmas as happy as possible for her – and perhaps Laura would join us? I'd be very pleased to have her.'

'That's a good idea,' Julian smiled. 'I've been worrying about leaving her alone in the cottage when I go.'

'That's settled, then, she'll come to us and have a family Christmas.'

Laura smiled wanly. It seemed her life was being arranged for her and she was too tired to protest – not that she wanted to. Christmas with the Herons and Sally would be much better than Christmas alone in the cottage or in her riverside apartment. The only thing that would make it perfect would be if Julian could be here as well. But now that she knew the full story she doubted if that were possible.

They watched him go out of the room and then Amanda took Laura's hand. She looked grave. 'You're being very brave – are you sure you want to go back to the cottage? You could stay here you know.'

'No, I've got to be there. With the fire going and the lights on at night it's obvious that the cottage is inhabited. If anyone should call, Julian would be trapped.'

'If you hadn't turned up Julian was going to live rough there – no lights and no proper fires. He could do that again.'

'It's too late. Mrs Charlton in the village shop knows that I'm there – she thinks I've got a friend with me. If she doesn't see any signs of life she'll be sure to send her husband up to see that everything's OK.'

Amanda shook her head. 'I can see you're determined, but, Laura, why are you doing this? You don't have to help Julian. You could make a run for it now – go straight to the police.'

'Not after everything Julian's just told me – that might put Sally in danger.'

'As I said before, you're a brave girl – but there's another reason why you want to help, isn't there?'

'What do you mean?' Laura felt herself flushing under Amanda's kindly scrutiny.

'You don't have to tell me, dear, but I know.' Amanda hugged her briefly and got up and went over to the door. 'I'll leave you alone a moment, Laura. I've just remembered there's something I want to give Julian. Something I found in the glove compartment of Geraldine's car after he'd gone.'

So it was obvious then. Obvious to Amanda, at least, that Laura was in love with Julian. She must be, to contemplate going back willingly to the cottage with him.

Some people would think she was crazy. After all, he could be going to take her back there to murder her. Everything he had told her about drug barons murdering his wife could have been a lie. It sounded pretty far-fetched, she had to admit. And yet it was true that he was an investigative journalist and he had been working on a television programme about drug-smuggling. He had annoyed some very dangerous people and he had received threats against his life.

Julian had told her he'd ignored the threats and taken extra precautions. He'd never dreamed that because they could not find him, they would harm his wife. They had murdered Geraldine, not Julian, and he felt responsible.

He believed that his activities had placed his family in danger. That was why he had had to remove Sally from London and place her in hiding.

He explained that if he gave himself up, it might take too long to convince the police of his innocence and, meanwhile, whoever had killed Geraldine might harm Sally and vanish without trace.

He had hoped that if he stayed away from the scene, the police would eventually uncover certain clues and trace the real culprits. But they had covered their tracks too well; the police still had no reason to suspect that anyone but the missing husband was involved.

Julian had decided to return to London, where he would try to initiate some action. He would not tell either Laura or Amanda exactly what he was going to do.

'Where's Amanda?'

Julian had returned; he was carrying their coats and boots.

'She just went to get something – something she found in the car.'

Amanda entered the room at that moment carrying a slim leather book – a diary. She looked uneasy.

'Julian, I hope you'll forgive me but I've

read this.'

He looked puzzled. 'What is it?'

'It's Geraldine's diary – there's nothing personal – just appointments – dentists, aerobic classes and the like. But there are dinner and theatre engagements too...'

'I don't understand, Amanda. Why did you find it necessary to go through it?'

Amanda flushed and Laura felt sorry for her.

'Julian, believe me I wasn't being nosy. But I thought that, from what you told me, Geraldine must have let her murderers into the house – you said there was no sign of a break-in – the b-body was in the sitting-room, not the hallway. It follows she must have known her murderer–'

'That's ridiculous – how could she know the sort of evil scum that are mixed up in the drugs trade!'

'No – listen, Julian. They're clever – you've said that yourself. What if the person who killed her got to know her first – somehow got an introduction so that he knew her socially?'

Julian was frowning considering Amanda's words. 'OK – but how does looking through her diary help?'

'The social engagements – we have a lot of

friends in common, haven't we? So I went through and found the usual names – people we both know. But there are some others, initials only, that I don't know at all.'

'Geraldine was very popular – she had friends that even I didn't know and I was married to her!'

'I know – so we're no further forward. But take the diary – look at the names and dates. They might mean something to you – you might recognize a name from your investigations – surely it's worth a try.'

'Thanks, Amanda. You're a good friend.' Julian pocketed the diary and soon they were wrapped up warmly against the cold pre-dawn air and taking their leave.

It was freezing hard and the roads were treacherous. Laura was glad that she was not driving and that they did not have far to go.

Soon they would be back at the cottage. She knew she was being selfish but she was glad they were going to be alone once more. She did not know exactly how much time they had left together, but she was beginning to suspect that the memories of it might have to last a lifetime.

TEN

'Tired, Laura?'

'A little.'

Julian was concentrating on his driving. As soon as they left the main road to take the mountain track he switched off the lights. Laura was surprised; surely now that she had provided a cover story about going to Carlisle to visit friends, Julian's original plan, of slipping away and back unnoticed, didn't matter?

Laura knew what the village shop was like for gossip – Ralph Latham would probably repeat what she had said and there would be no reason for anyone to question it. But then she noticed how anxiously Julian was watching the road – glancing in the mirror to see if there was anyone behind them – and she remembered the way he had left her in the car and searched the cottage after their shopping expedition.

Suddenly, she felt chilled to the bone. He was worried in case they were being followed – and not by the police. He must also have considered the possibility that the cottage was being watched. That someone could be watching and waiting for the opportunity to – to what?

Laura shivered.

Once more he seemed to have read her mind. 'Don't worry, Laura, it won't be for much longer and as soon as I'm gone you're to go straight back to Heron's Court, OK?'

'Heron's Court? I didn't know it was called that.'

'Yes, it's been in Douglas's family for centuries. He inherited the title and the estate quite young, which is why he decided to stay in the north of England. With his qualifications he could have made a fortune in the States but he had responsibilities to the land and his workers and tenants.'

'But he's still a doctor?'

'He's attached to a big hospital in Newcastle, but he also takes a couple of clinics over in Whitehaven, so living here, in the middle, suits him fine. He's at a conference in Edinburgh at the moment but you'll be meeting him soon.'

They had reached the cottage and Julian drove straight into the old barn. As he got out of the car, he said, 'Laura, I want you to–'

'I know. You want me to wait here, while you case the joint!' She grinned up at him and was relieved to see his answering smile. She felt nervous but she was determined to control it – humour helped.

He was back soon. The cottage was exactly as they had left it except, of course, that the fire was out. Julian busied himself at the hearth whilst Laura hurried through to the kitchen to fill the kettle.

By the time the sky had lightened to leaden grey, they were sitting on the old sofa sipping mugs of hot, sweet tea. Neither of them was hungry and the toast that Laura had made was left uneaten on the table.

'I'm very selfish, bringing you here.' Julian looked at her anxiously.

'We've been over all that – you didn't bring me – I wanted to come with you. In fact, you couldn't have stopped me.'

'I don't deserve such loyalty; not from someone whose life I've turned topsy-turvy like this.'

'Oh, it's not loyalty,' Laura tried to keep the tone of her voice light-hearted. 'I just wanted to keep an eye on my property – didn't you realize that?'

Julian laughed and pulled her into his arms.

'Hey – watch out – you'll spill my tea–' she gasped.

'Give it to me. Now, I'll just put it down here – carefully – and then … then, I'll carry on where I left off…'

His arms closed around her and his lips came down on hers. Laura shut her eyes as she gave herself to his embrace. The kiss was gentle at first, and then his fervour grew and Laura felt his lips moving more urgently; forcing hers to open to allow his tongue to probe the sweetness of her mouth. Laura felt her heart pounding. The growing warmth from the fire matched the heat spreading throughout her body. She moaned softly and then almost cried out in distress when Julian tore his lips away from hers.

He left one arm around her waist to support her and stroked her brow, gently, with his other hand.

His voice was sharp. 'You're burning up, Laura!'

'Mmm? What do you mean?' She raised her hands to her temples. With her fingertips she could feel her pulse throbbing.

Julian captured her hands and kissed her palms, then her fingers. 'You're burning, sweetheart – and not with passion for me,' he laughed ruefully. 'I think you've got a temperature. Of course – Amanda told me you had – hours ago, and in my selfishness, I clean forgot!'

He stood up and lifted her up into his arms and then he carried her upstairs like a child.

'What are you doing?'

'I'm taking you up to bed, my darling. Don't worry, you're only going to sleep and rest until you feel better – and I'm going to look after you.'

The bedclothes were cool and Laura welcomed the feel of them against her aching limbs. Julian had vanished while she slipped her clothes off and her nightdress on; now he re-appeared carrying a bowl of tepid water, a flannel and a huge towel.

'What's that for?'

'I'm going to bathe you with this water – cool you down. Lift up and slip this towel underneath you to save the bedclothes.'

When he had finished sponging her face, neck and arms, he was satisfied that she was a little cooler. He dried her out of the bed, then covered her with the bedclothes.

'I'm going downstairs to rake down the fire and put the guard up, then I'll bring you up a cool drink of squash and some aspirins. I don't think you've got anything more serious than a cold but what you need is a good, long sleep.'

He hadn't closed the curtains and, as she lay back amongst the pillows, Laura could see out across the fells.

The snow was no longer smooth. It was mottled and pitted where the thaw had begun, but then, as the air had got colder again, it had frozen into banks and ridges. It was a strange, surreal landscape, divided by ancient walls and dotted with hardy, leafless trees weathered into angry shapes.

Laura's eyes were hurting. She closed them and turned her head away from the light. She had not heard him return but she became aware that Julian was closing the curtains and then a strong arm slid under her back and raised her up.

'Drink this – just sip it – and take these tablets.'

'Yes, Doctor.' He was being so masterful that it made her giggle, but she did as she was told and then he eased her down again and turned to go.

'Julian – where are you going?'

'I'll be just across the landing – in your parents' room. You only have to call out if you need me.'

'But you might not hear me – you'll be asleep–'

'Don't worry, I sleep lightly.'

'Julian – don't leave me – I need you now–'

She heard the floorboard creak as he came back to the bed. Quickly, he stripped off his top layers of clothes and, lifting the bed-clothes, he slipped in beside her.

'You'll be all right you know,' she murmured as he took her in his arms.

'What are you talking about?'

She smiled as she snuggled up against him. 'You'll be quite safe with me, Doctor, I only want to sleep…'

It was not even noon, but outside the cottage the sky darkened. Laura's breathing became soft and regular and soon she was sleeping peacefully.

It began to snow again. Julian could see the shadows of the snowflakes drifting past the curtains and he worried. He could not afford to be snowed in now. He had to get back to London.

Laura sighed contentedly and moved in his arms. He turned towards her and tightened his hold. If only he could stay here – stay with this sweet girl whose valiant, trusting nature had done so much to restore his faith in humanity.

Well, no one could take this time away

from him. He bent his head and kissed her brow gently. She smiled ... he drifted off to sleep.

When Laura woke up she was disorientated. She remembered, only, that she had been feeling ill and, at first, she lay with her eyes closed and mentally examined her state of health. Her limbs had stopped aching and so had her head. She no longer felt hot and uncomfortable so her temperature must have gone. She was obviously better – she sighed contentedly.

The sigh produced a movement beside her in the bed and Laura froze with fright. Cautiously she put out a hand and it met a solid, human body. Memory came flooding back and she relaxed – but only slightly. Had she really asked Julian North to share her bed? Laura was mortified when she remembered that she had. She must have been much more feverish than she had imagined!

She moved her head on the pillow and half opened her eyes to squint upwards. He was sitting up reading from a slim, leather-bound book. Laura recognized the diary that Amanda had given them before they left Heron's Court: Geraldine's engagement diary.

He was turning the pages and frowning, and Laura looked at him surreptitiously. His strong, dark hair was tousled and the hair on his powerfully muscled chest was as vigorous as his beard. His skin was tanned from his time abroad.

There was no questioning his dark, good looks and no questioning how attracted to him she was. Laura suppressed a sigh – in her present situation such thoughts were dangerous.

He had not noticed that she was watching him and her gaze moved beyond him to take in the details of the room. She was puzzled. The curtains were open and bright sunlight streamed in through the window.

It had been morning when she had gone to sleep; a dull, overcast morning with the sky full of threatened snow.

'You've slept right round the clock – we both have.' He was smiling down at her. 'It was snowing when we went to sleep, but luckily the fall mustn't have lasted long.'

'Why "luckily"?'

'Remember, I have to leave soon? I don't want the roads to be blocked again.'

Laura turned her head away from him and he slid down in the bed and took her in his arms. 'I'm sorry, Laura.'

'Sorry? What for?'

'Sorry for everything – this whole great mess, but I promise you I'll get out of your life soon. You'll be able to forget all about me.'

She kept her head turned away from him and tried to stop the tears from squeezing out from under her eyelids. Was that what he thought she wanted – to forget all about him? Was that what he wanted? Was the closeness they had shared all to be put down to propinquity, after all?

'Feeling hungry?'

To her surprise, Laura discovered that she was and she turned towards him, opened her eyes and nodded.

'Right, I'll go down and make you a cup of tea and then, while you get ready I'll make breakfast.'

He was already out of bed and pulling on his jeans and tee-shirt. Before he left the room he straightened the bedclothes and, as he did so, the diary fell to the floor. He picked it up, put it in his pocket and would have left the room without comment but Laura called him back.

'Did you find anything useful in the diary?'

He turned to stare at her.

'I saw you going through it before. You were frowning – I – I'd like to know if you found anything that could help. After all, I can't help being interested in the outcome.'

Julian's voice was troubled. 'I suppose I should tell you. You've helped me willingly and I owe it to you – but I've never been one to burden other people with my problems.'

'Sometimes it's more of a worry to be kept in the dark,' she said. He stared at her bleakly and she smiled. 'Have you always been the strong silent type?'

She was rewarded with a grin. He came back to sit on the bed. 'Over the years my nearest and dearest have been known to criticize me for being uncommunicative. I suppose it's because I talk for a living that I tend to switch off when I get home. I realize how annoying that must be.'

'Not to say infuriating.'

'My, you are feeling better, aren't you? I'll go and get your breakfast.'

Laura lunged out and grabbed him. 'Julian, I'm serious, I really want to know if you've found anything in your wife's diary that will help you.'

Immediately, he became serious. 'OK, I'll tell you. I may have discovered something but I'm just not sure.'

169

He took hold of both of her hands and went on. 'It was easy for the police to suspect me. Anyone who knew us well would have been able to tell them that Geraldine and I had a stormy marriage – oh, it looked good on the surface – she was an accomplished actress and could put on a great show of being the devoted wife. But there had been gossip. Once they started investigating, the police would think they had a classic case of a jealous husband losing control and murdering his wife.'

Laura stared at him in consternation. She remembered his words on the night she had tried to run away – the night she had pretended that she was concerned about Steve. What had Julian said? 'Yes, I've been in love, Laura. I know what terrible things love can make you do.'

She could see what it was costing him to tell her about Geraldine. No wonder he had felt sorry for Maxine. It seemed as if he knew from personal experience the terrible pain inflicted by an unfaithful partner.

He was holding her hands tightly. 'Now that I've told you this, Laura, have you changed your mind? Do you still think I'm innocent of murder?'

Suddenly, she moved forward into his

arms. 'Of course, you're innocent. I could never doubt you.'

'But it's still my fault, you know.'

'Why? Why do you say that?'

'Because I wasn't there to look after her. To look after my wife and my child. I have to say this for her – no matter what her feelings were for me, she loved Sally. I had no qualms about leaving her in Geraldine's care.

'But there's no doubt in my mind that the people I annoyed in the course of my investigations into drug-trafficking were responsible for Geraldine's death and – who knows? – if Sally hadn't run upstairs and hidden in her toy cupboard, she might have been murdered too. It's too awful to contemplate.' Julian groaned and held Laura more tightly. She could feel him shaking.

'Don't even think about it – Sally's safe.'

'Only for the moment. Laura, I've got to stop them finding her. Somehow, I've got to point the police in the right direction. If I simply give myself up, I don't think they'd take anything I said seriously. They'd think I was concocting a story to protect myself.'

'What are you going to do?'

'Amanda may have hit on something when she suggested that Geraldine's killer got to know her socially – wormed his way into her confidence and into our home. There are some clues in the diary but I'll have to get back to London to follow them up. That's as much as I can tell you, at the present time, Laura. It might put your life in danger if you know too much – and if anything happened to you, my darling, I would never forgive myself.'

ELEVEN

The next few days developed a routine and atmosphere all of their own. Laura and Julian would share the basic household tasks, make meals, talk about anything except their problems and listen to the hourly news bulletins on the radio. There were no new developments and, eventually, the 'Belgravia murder' dropped out of the news schedules altogether.

Laura and her fugitive guest enjoyed an easy companionship but they never shared a bed again. In fact, Julian returned to sleeping downstairs by the fire. He didn't say so but she knew it was for reasons of security.

One day they went shopping in the village. Julian stayed in the car with the hood of his parka pulled well forward and Laura dashed into the general store as if she were in a hurry.

Luckily, it was crowded with people doing extra shopping before the Christmas holiday and she was only able to exchange hasty greetings with Mrs Charlton as she paid for her purchases.

'Thanks for the Christmas card and decorations you put in with the groceries, Mrs Charlton. It was very kind of you.'

'That's OK, Laura, love. Remember you and your friend are welcome at our house for your Christmas dinner.'

'Oh, I meant to tell you, we've been invited to Julia's friend's house in Carlisle – we were through there the other day.'

'Yes, Ralph Latham told me he'd seen you setting off. He was worried about you. It was late and the roads were bad. He was relieved when he noticed your car coming back early the next morning.'

Well, Laura thought, just as we suspected, nothing goes unnoticed in this village. I'm glad we decided I should mention in advance that I have plans for Christmas. We don't want anyone coming to visit the cottage, no matter how friendly their motives are.

When they got back they built up the fire and they feasted on crusty bread with ham and cheese, shortbread and fresh percolated coffee. Outside the skies glowered with the promise of bad weather to come but it never actually snowed.

'Do you realize that we're missing all the

fun of the seasonal television programmes?' Julian glanced up from one of the newspapers they'd bought and grinned.

'Strange to say, I haven't missed television at all,' Laura replied. 'But then, I don't usually have much time to watch. When I'm working on my designs at home I like to have the radio on or play my tapes.'

She frowned; something had been nagging away in her mind for some days and now she remembered what it was. 'Julian, what will happen to your programme? The one you've been working on about drug trafficking?'

'I'll go ahead with it. I'm more determined than ever to expose these evil men.'

'I can see why, but won't that be difficult?'

'Very. But Nick Harvey, my cameraman, has all the films, tapes and notes that we need. I'll contact him as soon as I get back to London and we'll start the editing and putting it all together.'

'Won't that be dangerous?'

'No, Nick and I have worked in some very dicey situations in the past – we trust each other completely. In fact, we'd already made emergency plans.'

Laura bit her lip anxiously.

'Don't worry, love. Nick would never

betray me to the police – or anyone else. While he's guarding all this information he's been keeping a low profile. Otherwise he would have been helping me with this other dreadful business.'

There was so much about Julian that she did not know. She had seen him on television, but his private life, until the moment their paths had crossed so dramatically, had been so different from hers.

One afternoon they settled down to read by the fire. Laura had chosen one of her mother's paperback detective stories and Julian was going over and over various clippings he had cut from the second lot of newspapers they'd bought. Laura went back to her book but could not summon enough concentration to follow the storyline, let alone spot the clues and attempt to solve the mystery.

That night Julian asked her what she was going to do when the holiday was over.

'I'll go back to work,' Laura replied. 'I've been thinking over what you said about Maxine and Steve. You're right, I don't think she'll carry out her threat now that she thinks she's rescued Steve from my clutches–'

'Does she only think she's rescued him? Would you have him back?' Julian's voice was sharp.

'I wouldn't have him if he came crawling!'

Julian laughed softly and pulled her into his arms.

'That's my girl,' he murmured.

Laura backed away abruptly and went into the kitchen to make some tea. She knew that what he said was only a figure of speech – a meaningless but affectionate phrase. If only he knew how much she would like that to be true – if only he had meant it when he had said, 'That's my girl'.

Next morning they watched from the landing window as the red van came up the track towards the cottage. As the van drew nearer, Julian moved to the side so that he was hidden by the curtain and Laura went downstairs.

She glanced round quickly to check if there were any signs of a masculine presence and, when she was satisfied that there were none, she opened the door and said hello to the postman. It was only courtesy to do so when he had driven all the way up the mountain track to deliver one letter.

He smiled as he handed over her mail and Laura exchanged Christmas greetings with him. She had to force herself to stand, calmly, in the doorway and give a cheery wave as he drove off.

Then she closed the door and leant against it nervously. They had been expecting one envelope and she knew what it would contain but the postman had left two and that was worrying.

Julian was coming down the stairs. 'What's the matter?'

Wordlessly, she held the envelopes out towards him. He examined them closely, holding them up to the light and even sniffing them.

'Do you mind if I open them?'

'Of course not – why should I mind?'

He managed a slight grin. 'They're both addressed to you.'

But he opened them anyway. The larger envelope first. It was an expensive and tasteful Christmas card from Amanda and Douglas Heron. Amanda had scrawled on the back:

Dear Laura,
Douglas joins me in hoping that you'll spend Christmas with us.
Regards,
Amanda Heron

This was the message that they had been

waiting for. The bit about wanting Laura to join them for Christmas was genuine, but it also meant that Douglas had returned from Edinburgh and he would take Julian back to London in his car.

The police were no longer searching cars, particularly cars going back to London and, in any case, it was unlikely that they would stop Sir Douglas Heron's distinctive Silver Shadow anywhere north of the Humber. As they got further south poor Julian would have to conceal his large frame in the boot. Fortunately, there was plenty of room in the boot of a Rolls.

Julian was opening the other envelope and Laura watched anxiously. Who else knew she was here? She was relieved when he smiled and held out a cheery Christmas card.

'Who's it from?'

'See for yourself.'

The card was from Ralph Latham. He, too, had scrawled a message on the back. He hoped that Laura and her friend would be staying in the area for New Year. There would be quite a few parties he could take them to. He reminded her that in this part of the world 'Hogmanay' was celebrated just as energetically as it was over the border in Scotland.

Laura laughed and Julian smiled and hugged her.

'You should take him up on that offer, even if your mythical friend "Julia" will be unable to accompany you. It seems to me young Ralph Latham is just what you need after the miserable Steve.'

She scowled and pushed him away. 'You'd like that wouldn't you?'

'Laura, why are you looking at me like that and what on earth do you mean?'

'I mean it would suit you fine to pass me on to Ralph, just like a parcel, so you can go off to London and forget about me!'

She ran upstairs, forgetting about her weak ankle until a vicious stab of pain made her cry out with rage and hurt.

She flung into her own room, slammed the door then threw herself on her bed. She waited for the sound of his footsteps coming up after her but there was only silence. He did not follow her. Laura collapsed sobbing amongst the pillows.

The day wore on and, eventually, the most delicious smell of cooking wafted up the stairs to tantalize her.

She wanted to go down but she did not know how she was going to face Julian. She was not ashamed of her feelings but, on reflection, the way she had behaved made her realize more than ever that there was a gulf between them.

She went into the bathroom and splashed cool water on her face and brushed her hair. She was hesitating at the top of the stairs when he appeared at the bottom and called up, 'There you are. I wish you would come down – I can't possibly eat all this food myself!'

Laura laughed and went down.

At the bottom he took hold of her hand and drew her over to the table. He had set it for a meal and decorated it with a new candle and the pine cones.

'I'm afraid it's pasta again and this time the sauce owes everything to what I could find in tins. My cooking skills are limited when we can't get out and buy fresh food every day.'

'I don't mind, it still smells delicious!'

He held her chair for her and Laura sat down.

'Would madam like to start with fruit juice? It came all the way from the carton in the fridge!'

Julian set out to humour her and they chatted inconsequentially across the table as they ate their meal. This time they drank a sparkling white wine that he had chilled in the fridge while he was cooking.

When he placed the cheese, biscuits and coffee on the table, Laura went to get a bottle of brandy and some glasses from the cupboard under the stairs. She had suddenly realized that this might be their last meal together – she might as well make the most of it.

She cupped her glass and sipped the brandy slowly, savouring the flavour. Then she smiled shyly at him. 'Thank you for not mentioning what happened before.'

Julian reached over and took her hand. 'I hope you don't really think I want to palm you off on young Latham?'

'I don't know what to think.'

Julian still had hold of her hand and he gripped it more tightly. 'Laura, there's something I must say. However Geraldine behaved, whatever she did, she didn't deserve to die like that. I believe that I am responsible for her death – no, listen to me. I also believe that anyone I am close to could be in danger. Do you understand?'

Laura pulled her hand away from his. 'Yes.'

'So do you also understand that I'm not

free to say any more than that?'

Laura nodded miserably but he went on, 'And, Laura, we've got to face the possibility that I may never be in a position to follow my heart. The one consolation is that you're young and lovely – you won't have to sit around waiting for an old codger like me!'

Laura was indignant. 'You're not old! Why, you can only be–' She searched his face. It was the first time she had thought about his age and it was very difficult to make a judgement when he had that beard.

'I'm thirty-two and you – well, if you've just finished college you must be about twenty-one.'

'I'm twenty-two.' She sounded so defiant that, suddenly, they both laughed.

He got up, stretched, and walked over to the fire. 'I'll put another log on and then you sit and relax whilst I do the dishes. No, I insist. I want you to remember me as being a good house-guest. Who knows? One day you may be able to invite me here again.'

It was after midnight when Julian kissed her goodbye and left the cottage to go to Heron's Court. He left it so late because he wanted to be sure that he would meet no revellers walking home from the village pubs to the outlying farms.

He went on foot across the fells, carrying his rucksack and looking very much the same as he did when he had arrived. Only then, the cottage had been cold and empty. Now it was warm and full of memories.

For a while he had had a refuge – a safe haven. Now he was a fugitive again.

Laura put out the lights, locked the doors and settled herself amongst the cushions on the sofa beside the fire. This was where Julian had slept.

She pulled the rug up to cover her and tried to sleep but her thoughts were following the man across the snowclad fells. She feared for him and yet she told herself that Julian North would be able to cope with whatever danger befell him. In her imagination she went with him every step of the way.

When dawn came the hearth was cold and Laura was still awake.

TWELVE

It was early summer and there were drifts of blossom on the hawthorn trees. Laura stood in the clearing and gazed around at the craggy oaks, sweet chestnuts and wild cherry. A tangled thicket of blackthorn barred her way to the lake and she turned and looked back along the woodland path towards the surrounding hills now iced only with moonlight.

She sighed and leant back against the trunk of an ancient oak. She could feel the cool, ridged bark through the thin fabric of her dress.

She could not go back, not yet. In the cottage she would be alone, imprisoned with her memories.

But the wood held memories, too.

This was where he had caught up with her when she had tried to escape. She remembered the moment of terror when she had seen him coming towards her. She had fainted and he had carried her back in his arms...

Suddenly there was a movement in the undergrowth and her heart quickened as the foliage parted, but it was only a young rabbit, more startled than she was. It stared at Laura with liquid eyes and then darted off to vanish into the sweet-scented shadows.

A cool wind lifted her hair. She heard a curlew calling long and low across the felltop. The wind strengthened and she shivered. It was time to go back.

The small fire she had left burning was still glowing cheerfully. She put on another log and went through into the kitchen to heat some milk.

Laura caught sight of herself in the mirror propped up on the windowsill. Her copper-coloured hair was as vibrant as ever but her creamy complexion was almost wax-like in its paleness. Her apple-green cotton dress brought out the colour in her eyes but, nevertheless, she looked tired and sad.

She poured the hot milk into a mug and spooned in some honey. It was not yet midnight; she would sit by the fire.

Laura turned on the radio and curled up on the sofa. She cupped her hands around the mug and tried to listen to the music but the thoughts she had been keeping at bay came back to torment her.

They had sat here together so many times in those few short days. Outside the cottage the winter landscape had been hushed and still. Inside there had been only the subdued crackling of the fire and the occasional hiss as a snowflake drifted down the chimney into the flames. She remembered the first time he had taken her in his arms...

The music stopped and the disc jockey announced they were going over to the newsroom. She reached out, quickly, and switched off the radio. She did not want to hear the news. Even to hear his name on the radio caused her too much pain.

The rising wind rattled the window panes and there was a sudden pattering of rain. Laura put her empty mug down on the floor and wrapped her arms around her drawn up knees. She stared into the flames. If only she could stop thinking about him. If only she could stop herself believing that one day he would come back.

The day after Julian had gone she had spent in tidying up the cottage. What food there was left she packed into the same cardboard boxes that she'd brought with her and she put them in the car. She raked out the

187

hearth and stripped her bed. The bedclothes would have to be washed the next time she came here. Finally, she fell exhausted on to the sofa and went to sleep.

She had meant only to rest for a few hours before setting off for Heron's Court, but she had had no sleep since Julian had gone and when she awoke she found it was early the next morning.

She pulled on her outdoor clothes and left without a backward glance. It was Christmas Eve.

The old house was fragrant with the smell of evergreens and the delicious aroma of festive cooking. Sally was pleased to see her and Amanda was grateful for her help both with the child and the preparations for the next day.

After Sally had gone to bed they relaxed with a glass of sherry and waited for Douglas to come home. They were tired and they sat in companionable silence.

Laura considered the relationship between Amanda Heron and Julian North. On the surface they seemed just like old friends but Laura wondered, once more, if this extremely attractive woman had ever regretted marrying the young medical student instead of her childhood friend.

They would make a handsome couple, Laura mused: Julian so tall and dark and powerful and Amanda, slender and sophisticated. She could not stop her mind from leaping ahead and allowing the possibility that, now that Julian was free from an unhappy marriage, he and Amanda would finally get together.

But she dismissed all such thoughts the minute Douglas Heron returned. It was obvious that he and Amanda were a more than usually happy couple. Whatever they were doing for Julian, they were doing out of loyal friendship.

He arrived in a flurry of snowflakes and cold air just as the bells started ringing in a distant church. He was as tall as Julian but blond and extremely distinguished. Amanda hurried straight into his arms.

'Douglas, I'm so glad you're home. How did it go?'

'All right. I don't want to say too much but Julian is in a safe place.'

Laura wondered whether Julian was staying with his cameraman friend, Nick Harvey.

'So you're Laura? Julian has told me so much about you and how grateful he is for your help. I'm glad you're to spend Christmas with us. By the way – do you realize that it's past midnight? Happy Christmas, Laura – and Happy Christmas, darling!'

He turned to his wife and kissed her. Laura suddenly felt utterly alone. She made her excuses and went up to bed. As she left the room Amanda disengaged herself and smiled at her. 'Good-night, Laura, dear. See you in the morning.'

Christmas Day had been as happy as they could make it for Sally. She had still not said anything about what happened the night her mother had died and it was obvious that she was missing her father. But when she found her presents under the tree, for a while, she was as pleased and excited as any normal child.

There was a doll's house from her father, Laura guessed that Amanda must have arranged that, and, also, she had made sure there were plenty of intriguing little parcels to open. Douglas had brought her a whole family of teddy bears from the famous Bear Den in Edinburgh.

There was even a present for Laura – a gift-wrapped collection of expensive toiletries.

'Not very original, I'm afraid,' Amanda apologized. 'But I had to do the shopping in such a hurry. I took Sally with me and, even though she was all bundled up in winter clothes, I kept imagining that someone would recognize her.'

They had asked Laura to stay on for New Year, but she resisted their entreaties and drove back to Newcastle. She told them that she wanted to get back to work on her new designs.

This was partly true, but also, no matter how kind and hospitable they were, she felt like an intruder. They were enjoying Sally's company so much. She was like the child they had never had. Laura knew that, so long as Sally was at Heron's Court, Julian would not have to worry about his daughter.

She saw the New Year in alone in her apartment. She could hear the cheerful racket coming from the clubs and wine bars on the quayside but she was not tempted to go and join in the fun or to seek out her friends from work.

She wondered what Julian was doing as the old year died. Was he thinking of her?

When she went back to work, the craft centre was the usual hive of activity and cheerful gossip. Everyone there was pleased to see her and it gave her a jolt to realize that none of them had any idea how much had happened to her since she had said goodbye to them a couple of weeks before Christmas.

'Hey – have you heard about Steve Fraser?'

Chris Martin, her boss, came over to her work bench.

'N-no, what's happened?'

'Don't look so worried,' Chris grinned. 'Apparently, he's left his firm and set up on his own. I know we're losing a valuable contact but – he may do us some good yet – when he becomes rich and successful!'

Laura wondered if Maxine would carry out her threat but as the weeks passed and the orders came in as usual she realized that Julian had been right. She hoped that Maxine had gone along with Steve's decision. It probably had not been good for him working for his father-in-law. She genuinely wished them well.

The 'Belgravia murder' had dropped out of the news altogether. There was no hint in the media whether the police were still searching for the missing husband or whether their investigations had changed course.

Then everything happened at once.

She came home from work one bitterly cold evening in February to hear the phone ringing. She hurried to her door, fumbling in her bag for her keys. She had never stopped hoping that Julian would get in touch – tell her how things were going. But it wasn't him.

'Laura, are you alone?'

Amanda's voice sounded so strained that Laura dropped her handbag and slowly sank to her knees.

'Yes, I'm alone.'

'I've been trying to get you for hours!'

'I worked late. Please tell me what's the matter!'

'Julian's programme is going to be on television tonight on Channel Four – straight after the news.'

Laura felt weak. 'And Julian – has he...?'

'He hasn't given himself up – he's still in hiding.'

'Has he been in touch with you?'

'A couple of times – to ask about Sally – and to tell us about the programme tonight. I said I'd let you know.' Amanda hurried on. 'He asked how you were. I told him we'd exchanged a couple of letters and that you seemed to be enjoying yourself back at work.'

Laura gripped the telephone table with her other hand. Her letters had been deliberately cheerful. She had not wanted to admit to Amanda how much she was missing Julian because, then, she would have to admit to herself how deep her feelings for him were.

'I've got to go,' Amanda said. 'Please keep in touch.' She rang off.

He had shaved off his beard. The man she saw doing the 'links' in the programme about drug-trafficking, was the man she remembered from previous television appearances. The programme was riveting. She had no idea how they had done it, but Julian and Nick Harvey had followed a single consignment of drugs on its journey from South East Asia to Africa then on to Amsterdam and finally to the United Kingdom.

The detective work, the interviews and the filming, some of it secret, were brilliant. Finally, Julian faced the camera and said, 'That was the story of how one consignment of heroin came to the British Isles. There will be many more.

'I intend to hand over a copy of this programme to the police – in person.'

Laura reached forward and switched off the set. So Julian was going to the police, himself. Did that mean that he had finally turned up enough evidence to trace the real murderer? Or did it mean that now that his programme had been televised he no longer had any valid reason to stay at liberty? She got up briskly; she was frightened of the direction her thoughts were taking.

When her radio alarm woke her up the next morning it was like a time warp. The news was full of the 'Belgravia murder' again. Breakfast television covered the story and the later editions of the newspapers carried it on their front pages.

Laura forced herself to go to work and tried to carry on as if nothing out of the way had happened.

For the next few days she neither ate nor slept properly and then, one day, as she was drinking coffee in the rest room at work, she heard on the lunch-time news that the evidence Julian North had uncovered for his television programme had enabled the police to round up some very dangerous criminals. Their careers in crime were over for a very long time.

Furthermore, he had been released from police custody; he was no longer suspected of the murder of his wife.

Laura's mug crashed to the floor and she dropped her head into her hands and wept uncontrollably.

'Feeling better, now?'

Chris was smiling at her. One of the other girls had gone hurrying to get him and he had lifted Laura up and carried her, bodily, into his office. He'd set her down in the one comfortable armchair.

He made her a cup of hot, sweet tea and, when she'd calmed down enough to drink it, he sat on the edge of his desk in front of her and began to talk.

'I know what's wrong with you, Laura.'

Her heart lurched but his next words reassured her.

'You've been working non-stop – did you realize that? When you first started work here, I knew you were still grieving for your parents. You didn't want to talk about it – you seemed to bottle it all up and just work harder and harder. Well, I think it's finally caught up with you – you need a break.'

'I've just had a break,' Laura said weakly.

'Yes, and you probably never set foot out of your apartment. I think you just shut yourself away and worked on your designs.'

If only he knew, Laura thought!

'Well, I'm going to see that you have a proper holiday this time. I've got an important order for leather jackets and I'm going to Devon to buy some veg-tanned hides. I know it seems a long way to go to buy leather but there's a nice little tannery, Baker's, in Colyton that does the traditional oak-bark tanning. You'd enjoy finding out more about the process.'

'Would I?' Laura smiled uncertainly through her tears.

'Yes – and I'd enjoy having you to keep me company. Once our business is over we'll find a good hotel and have a few days' holiday – my treat. Your new range of jewellery has been bringing in some lucrative orders so you needn't feel guilty.'

Suddenly, Chris laughed. 'If only you could see your face! Don't worry, Laura, love. I'm not planning to seduce you – I'm not foolish enough to get involved with my employees – no matter how attractive they are! Now, please say you'll come with me.'

She smiled ruefully. She had always liked Chris but she suddenly realized what a good-looking man he was. This trip might be just what she needed.

It was partly work, so it would help to stop her spending all her time wondering whether Julian would ever get in touch with her – especially now that he was free. But also, a few days spent in the company of a handsome and cultured man would be

197

extremely good for her ego. She agreed to go.

That had been four months ago. She had enjoyed the trip to Devon as much as possible in the circumstances. Chris was an entertaining companion and he was willing to share his knowledge and expertise in all aspects of his business.

One night, as they sat over a leisurely dinner in their hotel, Laura asked him why he was being so kind.

'I have to be honest, my motives weren't entirely altruistic. I needed someone to share the driving and, also, someone intelligent enough to be a genuine help with the business side. It's a bonus that you're also gorgeous to look at!'

They both laughed.

Later, alone in her hotel room, Laura listened to the news on the bedside radio. She learned that a man had been arrested for the murder of Geraldine North. Mrs North's diary had contained important clues.

When she got back to Newcastle there was a letter from Amanda waiting for her.

Dear Laura,
I have tried to contact you several times and, eventually, I phoned the workshop. I was

told you were in Devon with Chris Martin. Nevertheless, you might like to hear the background to what has been happening.

Geraldine's murder was nothing to do with Julian's exposé of the drug ring. She had been having an affair and, when she tried to break it off because Julian was coming home, her lover went to their home and made a scene. Their violent quarrel ended in her death.

Just before the news broke, Sally told me all she could remember. She had been woken up by angry voices and started to go downstairs. Her mother saw her and screamed at her to go back and hide but, before Sally turned and ran, she got a good look at the man who was menacing her mother. The poor child was able to identify him from photographs.

When Julian returned he found the body of his wife and searched the house, frantically, for his child until he found her sobbing in her toy cupboard.

The rest you know.

Yours sincerely,
Amanda Heron

Laura stared at the neat writing on the expensive paper. The word 'Nevertheless'

199

worried her. Had Amanda read some significance into the trip to Devon? Did she think there was something between Chris Martin and herself?

Laura was not able to find out. When she phoned Heron's Court, she was told that Lady Heron had gone to London and had left instructions that no one was to have her address. She guessed that it would be to do with Julian's case and that Sally would be with her.

Since then she had worked hard, started going out socially with her colleagues from the craft centre and had tried to enjoy herself.

Every time the phone rang she hoped it would be Julian but it never was. Eventually, even to see his name in newsprint became an exquisite form of torture. She stopped buying newspapers and switched off the television or radio when it was time for the news.

However, she could not avoid the headlines on the news stands when the case came to court and when it was time for the jury to retire and consider the verdict she asked for some time off work and fled to the cottage.

Now, sitting by the dying fire, she knew

what a mistake that had been. Every room was full of bitter-sweet memories. A few hours ago she had run out into the moonlit night and taken refuge in the wood but, even there, her heart had betrayed her.

When the hearth was cold Laura lay back amongst the cushions and closed her eyes. She prayed for sleep...

She was back in the wood but this time she went plunging through the thorn bushes until she reached the lake. She stood on the shore, her dress torn and her limbs scratched and bleeding.

As she looked out across the cold, grey waters a mist rose and surrounded her until only the tops of the surrounding trees were visible above her. Laura looked up and, raising her arms, she cried out for someone to come and find her. No one answered her entreaties and she felt herself slipping down into the mist.

The ground beneath her feet dissolved and she went down and down through the formless ether until someone caught her and held her in his arms.

Laura moaned and opened her eyes. The lake, the trees and the mist receded but the arms were still around her. She looked up and saw his face.

'Julian.'

'Laura, my darling, I've missed you so.'

As he kissed her she raised one hand and stroked his clean-shaven cheek wonderingly. When they paused for breath, she asked, 'How did you get in?'

'The same way as last time – you haven't fixed the locks yet.'

'How long have you been here?'

'I've just arrived. I left London as soon as the jury brought in the verdict. He was found guilty, by the way. I drove to Newcastle and when I couldn't get an answer at your apartment, I made a phone-call, and then I came on here.'

'Why did you come?'

'Because I love you – don't you know that?'

But Laura only frowned. 'Then, why have you never been in touch until now?'

Julian pulled her into his arms and held her close.

'At first I couldn't risk involving you in something that might prove to be very dangerous. And then, when it was obvious that Geraldine's murder was a private matter, I didn't want your name dragged through the headlines.

'Believe me, I wanted to phone you so

many times but Amanda told me you were enjoying being back at work and doing well. I thought you might be forgetting about me and, much as it hurt, I persuaded myself it would be better for you if you did.'

'I could never forget you – don't you know that?'

'And then Amanda told me you went on holiday with your boss–'

'It was a business trip!'

'I know – I asked him.'

'You did what?'

'That phone-call I made in Newcastle. Poor guy, it was the middle of the night, but he took it well. Oh, Laura, darling I couldn't stay away from you any longer but I had to be sure that there was no one else.'

'What on earth did you say to Chris?'

'Don't worry, I was very diplomatic – I said I was a friend of the family just returned from abroad and I wanted to know how you were getting on.'

'And Chris believed your story?'

'I think so. He said you'd asked for a few days' leave and talking to him convinced me that there was nothing more between you than friendship. I guessed where you'd be.'

Laura felt dazed. It was dawn and the cottage was cool. She shivered.

'Cold, sweetheart?'

Julian knelt by the hearth. It didn't take him long to get the fire going, then he rose and walked over to the window. 'Come here, Laura, look at this.'

The mist, rising from the lake, had seeped up through the wood and was swirling across the fell towards the cottage.

Julian put his arms around her. 'Amanda and Douglas are taking Sally back to Heron's Court. I told them we would meet them there.'

She looked up into his eyes and smiled. 'You were sure that I would go with you, then?'

'Will you?'

'Yes.'

'And, Laura, one day soon – when we've given ourselves time to put this nightmare behind us – will you marry me?'

'Yes.'

He held her close and they stood for a while just happy to be together. Then Laura turned her head to look out of the window. She smiled wonderingly. 'Looks like we're marooned again.'

The mist had completely surrounded the cottage, enclosing them in a silent, mysterious world.

Julian laughed softly. 'You're right, we can't leave until the mist clears.'

'What shall we do until then?'

Julian picked her up and carried her over to the sofa. 'We'll sit together by the fire.'

The publishers hope that this book has given you enjoyable reading. Large Print Books are especially designed to be as easy to see and hold as possible. If you wish a complete list of our books please ask at your local library or write directly to:

Dales Large Print Books
Magna House, Long Preston,
Skipton, North Yorkshire.
BD23 4ND

This Large Print Book, for people
who cannot read normal print,
is published under the auspices of

THE ULVERSCROFT FOUNDATION

... we hope you have enjoyed this book.
Please think for a moment about those
who have worse eyesight than you ...
and are unable to even read or enjoy
Large Print without great difficulty.

You can help them by sending a
donation, large or small, to:

**The Ulverscroft Foundation,
1, The Green, Bradgate Road,
Anstey, Leicestershire, LE7 7FU,
England.**
or request a copy of our brochure for
more details.

The Foundation will use all donations
to assist those people who are visually
impaired and need special attention
with medical research, diagnosis
and treatment.

Thank you very much for your help.